the daughters
of joy

The Seven Spiritual Laws of Success

The Return of Merlin

Boundless Energy

Perfect Digestion

The Way of the Wizard

Overcoming Addictions

Raid on the Inarticulate

The Path of Love

The Seven Spiritual Laws of Success for Parents

The Love Poems of Rumi
(edited by Deepak Chopra;
translated by Deepak Chopra and Fereydoun Kia)

Healing the Heart

Everyday Immortality

The Lords of the Light

On the Shores of Eternity

How to Know God

the daughters of joy

deepak chopra

G. P. PUTNAM'S SONS
NEW YORK

This is a work of fiction. Names, characters, places, and incidents either are the product of the author's imagination or are used fictitiously, and any resemblance to actual persons, living or dead, business establishments, events, or locales is entirely coincidental.

G. P. Putnam's Sons
Publishers Since 1838
a member of
Penguin Putnam Inc.
375 Hudson Street
New York, NY 10014

Library of Congress Cataloging-in-Publication Data

Chopra, Deepak.
Daughters of joy / Deepak Chopra.
p.   cm.
ISBN 0-399-14948-1
I. Title.
PS3553.H587D3   2002   2002068206
813'.54—dc21

Printed in the United States of America
1   3   5   7   9   10   8   6   4   2

This book is printed on acid-free paper. ∞

BOOK DESIGN BY SCJ DESIGN

To Tara, my daughter of joy

Love is not a mere sentiment.
It is the ultimate truth that lies at the heart of creation.

• *r a b i n d r a n a t h   t a g o r e* •

October 28

Dear Marty,

Here are the finished galleys for the book, with my heart-felt thanks. I know it was tough sledding at times, and more people than your boss will want to believe that Dolly and Elena are real only in my mind. Just remember our confidentiality agreement and don't be tempted to di-vulge their true identity. I won't mind having the last laugh if this gets dismissed as a hoax.

If by some amazing chance a royalty check drifts in, forward it to general delivery at my old post office in Boston. Who knows where I'll be a year from now? I'm writing this letter by a candle stub, and overhead a trillion stars are filtering through pine boughs. The first snow can't be far away. If you drive past a bunch of raggedy guys warming their hands over an oil drum, you'll know that the fourth one is me (inside joke, but I'm sure you get it).

All my best wishes,
Jess

o n e

"Love has found you."

My name is Jess Conover, and I didn't invent skepticism. Let me say that right away. Only as it happens, I was guilty of ignoring the signs and omens that must have been trying to get my attention for a long time. I don't blame myself. I'm just glad that I noticed a clue when I did. It cut across my path like a firefly in tall summer grass and teased me into chasing it. One second too late, and there would have been nothing to see.

When all this began, I was living in a one-bedroom apartment in the South End. It came with brown tiles in the bathroom, no visible creatures, and one outstanding feature that made up my mind—a large bay window that gets enough morning sun to incite optimism. I had been living alone since my girlfriend Renee moved out. I thought we were happy until the morning she left. She gave me a last kiss, told me it was nobody's fault, and took a box of books under her arm. Her brother came the next day with his van, and I helped him load the rest.

This event must have been one of the signs I missed. When I didn't ask for clarification, Renee didn't offer any, but once she was out of the house she seemed to like me better. We still talked all the time, and visiting privileges were reinstated on a limited basis. But in the four months since, I began to feel jumpy when I wasn't looking.

I turned twenty-eight in September. I was earning my way as a writer—or, to be completely accurate, a rewriter, which means that I took the rough copy churned out by reporters and turned it into a finished story. I worked for one of the free papers you can find in boxes outside the T and in any Starbucks around Boston. Being a rewrite man is like being a real writer, only not quite, just as reheating leftover spaghetti is like being a real chef, only not quite.

One Sunday morning in November I had settled back in the bay window to read the paper. Ideally, it would have been sunny, but a cloud bank had decided to move in from the sea to hang out over town.

My eye caught a printed item in the classifieds. It was by far the smallest ad on the page, a single line of type set in a box with a lot of white space around it. Despite myself, I felt a shiver.

Love has found you. Tell no one, just come.

The nine-word message (I counted) seemed totally out of place. The rest of the page was crammed with public notices such as bankruptcies and sheriff's auctions—matters of record, not of passion. Yet passion was what I'd stumbled upon. I found it very strange. More than that, I began to feel disturbed.

I had gotten up around eight that morning, trotted out for a French-roast-to-go at the café down the street, and flirted with the tattooed counter girl as I paid for my coffee. At the last minute I exchanged the *New York Times* for the *Globe*, because I had a dim notion about looking for a used bike. Usually I don't bother with the

classifieds. So you see how much trouble the universe was going to
to show that it had a sense of humor.

I decided to call Renee, who was in her old place by the Fenway. The phone rang six times before she picked up.

"I have to read you this thing," I said.

"Hold on a second." I could hear muffled yawns at the other end.

"I thought you'd be up by now," I said lamely, glancing at the
clock. Quarter to nine.

Renee's voice came back shaggy with sleep. "No, I still get up
after ten. A lot like I have every Sunday, right?"

"Right." In my mind's eye I saw her soft blue eyes opening
slowly and reluctantly and wisps of long blonde hair tangled around
her neck.

We had never been on the same schedule when we tried living
together. I would already be running in third or fourth gear by
eight in the morning while Renee was barely in first. I would be
fidgeting at the front door, impatient to hit the street, while she
was wandering the apartment with a blueberry Pop-Tart in one
hand and a toothbrush in the other.

"What's going on?" Renee had gotten out of bed and switched
to her portable phone.

I read aloud. *"Love has found you. Tell no one, just come."*

"Okay, but I should put on a top first." Renee was pretty quick
for a groggy person. I told her I had been quoting an ad in the paper. "Hold on," she said.

I could hear splashing sounds now and knew she was throwing
cold water over the back of her neck. Renee finds this necessary
before she can accept that she isn't going back to bed.

"Come on," I said, trying to cajole a reaction. "You don't think
it's weird? Some lonely soul names a secret rendezvous where
everyone can read it?"

"No one will care except whoever it's meant for," Renee said. "Who signed it?"

"Nobody. Wait, there's a number at the bottom. I don't know how I didn't see it before."

Yet the fact stood that when I first read it, I had only seen a single line of type surrounded by white space. "The number's in New Hampshire," I said, gathering that from the area code: 603. "And there's a set of initials. J. C."

"There you go. Someone threw out a message in a bottle, and it found the right person," Renee said.

"What do you mean?"

"They're your initials. Anyway, you jinxed it. You told me, and it says tell no one. Were the instructions too hard?"

I was irked. "You don't feel any vibe from this?" I urged. "I know you're curious."

"Like, not even a little, dude." Renee was twenty-seven, a year younger than me. But when she started reverting back to adolescence, it meant she wasn't having fun.

"Okay, I get it," I said, backing off. "I guess it's a prank. At best some local Romeo trying to show off."

"Some local Romeo who's a little too full of himself," Renee said briskly. She had wandered over to open a window, because I could suddenly hear traffic noise through the phone. It reminded me of how I used to plead with her not to keep the bedroom so hot at night. I would wake up in a sweat, throwing off the sheets just to be able to breathe.

"So, are you going to call the number?" she asked.

"You think I should?"

"Chances are you'll just be stepping into someone's private weirdness. You don't really see a story here, do you?"

It had been a long time since I'd chased after news stories—

I wasn't heading that way here. I don't really like hard news re-porting to begin with. It's too much like opening oysters, using a dull blade to crack someone's shell and expose their quivering misery.

"Look," I said. "Have a Pop-Tart, brush your teeth. Sorry I dumped you out of bed."

"Just remember to take a coat. New Hampshire's already frozen in."

"I haven't even called yet."

There was a pause at the other end. "Well, I know you, and I know that tone of voice."

I heard myself laugh, one of my nervous laughs when I feel busted. "You should go with me. We might have an adventure," I said, giving it one last shot.

"This conversation has been enough of an adventure, sweetie. I'll call you."

"Okay, good."

I hung up and considered what to do next. To tell you the truth, talking to Renee had made me even more jumpy. I could usually work my jitters out physically, and without killing myself I had ended up with a solid bod. Renee called it my wall. After we began to go out and could really talk, she told me I was lucky that we met on a blind date. "You didn't look like you had a sensitive bone in your body," she said, as if sensitivity has a weight limit and I was going way over. I'm not huge, but you could imagine me out rowing on the river before work. Dress me up and I can be mis-taken for someone sporting an MBA. Myself, I liked the wall. It had its advantages.

I looked outside and saw that it was beginning to snow. It wasn't really coming down yet, just enough to muffle my view of the street. I could see cars sliding as they rounded the corner beneath my window. I put on my gray sweats and a pair of beat-up Nikes that I trust. When I got downstairs the snow had caused the wind to subside. I ran at a fast clip, appreciating the sharp pang of frigid air entering my lungs. The early snow looked like powdered sugar on the streets, deceptively innocent until I slipped on a nasty patch of black ice crossing Mass. Ave. I lunged forward, barely catching myself on my hands, which got scraped raw. A car whizzed by inches from my face, honking with alarm. The close call didn't scare me, but I didn't need the rush, either. Now I was twice as jumpy. I listened to the pulse pounding in my ears the whole way home.

Entering the apartment, my eyes were still dazzled with snow glare. When they cleared, the first thing I saw was the folded newspaper lying on the window seat where I had left it. Absently I walked over and picked it up again. The nine-word item was still there, six inches down on the far right. With my fleece sweats, I wiped the exercise sweat from my face and then reached for the phone.

It rang many times—I stopped counting after ten. At the last moment, just before I gave up, a voice said, "Yes?"

This monosyllable came through the line faintly, with a quaver, and it threw me off. I never imagined that the message of passion could have been from an old lady, but there was no mistaking an old lady's voice. "I'm calling about your ad in the paper?" I said hesitantly.

After a moment the quavery voice said, "You saw it. Good. Now you should come here."

"You might not understand. I'm not answering the ad," I said.

"Yes, you are."

The voice sounded older than my grandmother, who died when she was eighty-three. I looked out at the snow, which was thicker now, pale oatmeal flakes falling steadily from the sky.

"Are you the one who placed the ad?" I said.

"That's not really relevant, is it?" she said more sharply. "What's relevant is that you noticed. You'd better start out now. They say this storm is going to turn bad before long." There was a silence before she added, "It is you, isn't it?"

"Who do you think I am?" I said cautiously.

"Someone who wants the message to be for him," she said. "And someone who's also afraid that the message *is* for him."

It was a surreal moment, a turning point. I don't expect you to get that, not just yet. The normal thing would have been to tell her that I wasn't going to cross state lines on a long, cold trip just because a stranger dared me to. "My car's too old. I'll get stuck," I said, hearing how feeble that sounded.

The old lady laughed in a short burst that was almost a bark. "Tell yourself that you're coming up for human interest. I'm human, though it's far from the interesting part." She started giving me directions to her house without explaining how she knew I was a writer.

"Wait, you're jumping way ahead," I said, getting more nervous.

"Why are you arguing?" she asked. "The story wants to play it-self out, doesn't it?"

Things might have ended there despite her insistence. I might have ignored the provocation. Because it was true enough that my car could wind up in a ditch on an unlit back road. But the old lady cut my thoughts short by raising her voice a notch and speaking very precisely. *"Four men were standing around the bonfire warming their hands that night. Only one of them knew he was an angel."*

In fifteen minutes, I found myself heading north to New Hampshire. To explain why, I have to back up.

Sixteen was the worst year of my life. I shot up three inches that year, my frame telescoping faster than my muscles could keep up with. I was fumbling and uncoordinated on the field, any field, no matter what sport I tried out for. But that didn't make it the worst year of my life.

To understand why it earned that honor, you have to know that I was hanging on by a thread as the new kid in a backwater town in the Deep South. Ohio wasn't home anymore, because my father had accepted a sudden job transfer. A series of bad accidents had injured some workers, mostly black, in a decaying textile mill owned by his company, and they needed a new manager. Even though it meant pulling me and my sister Linny out of school, my dad made the move. We drove the whole way to Georgia with me burying my head in my arms, shut down completely. I wouldn't eat or get out to stretch my legs or talk like a human being.

We arrived in a one–Wal-Mart county, as locals put it. The town itself had been bypassed by the interstate forty years earlier, and I became an outsider overnight. The poor black kids, seizing on sports as their only way out, killed me at basketball. I tried to find another way to hold my head up, and when I got equally killed at football, I drifted to long-distance running, which no one seriously considered a sport. There was minimal communication between me and the other refugees to track and field, but then my isolation took an unexpected twist.

Coursing the miles of rutted lanes overgrown with live oaks and yellow pine, I began to imagine. I didn't know why, except it was either that or let the demon of despair eat me for lunch. At first I invented carnal scenes involving myself and an unattainable blonde girl, a senior, who in my fantasy gave me the precious gift of saying yes. Gradually, though, I began to notice other raw material. Not an inner thigh or the outline of a bra. Not even carnality. The landscape around me had always looked deserted on my solitary runs, but now I could populate it. I found stories in the derelict farms ruined by history and the woods fragrant with tanbark and ferns. I called up the shapes of soldiers long gone; I loaded cannon and survived the hundred-year flood that devastated my cotton. Once I was home, I wrote down what the land had told me.

As I filled the external emptiness with fictions, I filled myself. Inventing my longest and most ambitious story occupied two months of junior year. It was called "The World's Greatest Lover." The plot isn't important, although I could still recite it by heart. In fact I did so then, as I was driving to New Hampshire in the snowstorm. Peering through my windshield as the wipers shoveled aside the fat wet flakes, my first true fiction returned as vividly as the day I wrote it.

Once there was a forgotten man who lived in the basement of a church. He was gnome-like and for all practical purposes invisible to others. His job was to take care of the furnace and sweep up after mass was over. Then one day the man suffered a heart attack. When the medics arrived at his apartment and took him away on a stretcher, breathing but near death, they saw that the walls were plastered with pictures of women. There was also a kind of primitive altar with stubs of candles that had been used for services.

The church officials were disturbed, and when he recovered, they informed him he was fired. The man found himself on the street and was never thought about again. Except that the youngest priest, as he started stripping the offending pictures off the wall, noticed something everyone had overlooked in their outrage. The photos were all of unwed mothers, homeless women, victims of abuse and tragedy. Reluctantly the heads of the church were won around to the view that their invisible gnome was innocent. A search was started to give the forgotten man back his home, but he had disappeared off the face of the earth.

I decided my story was good enough to show to somebody. So

I found myself reading it standing up in English class on creative writing day. There was silence when I got through, and for a moment I was amazed that everyone could be so moved by words I'd written. Then a voice from the back started tittering, and someone else pretended to sob with loud sniffles that made several girls laugh.

The horror struck me. In their minds I had offered iron proof that I was a girl. Compared to this, long-distance running was nothing. I could only suck up the shame until my weight caught up with my height and I was able to pound a few of them. "You're lucky they don't think you're a faggot," my coach said when he pulled two of us apart. None of it mattered. I had found my life's aspiration, though to tell the truth I came to doubt it later when I moved north and discovered what brilliant pens could truly do.

Here's the point. In the last paragraph of the story, there was a coda. The gnome-like man had found his way to an empty lot where the homeless gather. By this time he was too weak from exposure to do anything but lie on the ground drifting in and out of consciousness. In his mind, some of the women from the photos were standing in a circle to keep the predators off.

Four junkies stood around a barrel warming their hands over a fire made of newspapers and kerosene rags. They didn't notice that behind them the gnome from the church basement was dying.

Then a blinding light caused them to fall to their knees with fear. An angel had swooped down to fetch the dying man—or so the junkies claimed. Passersby only remembered a police helicopter shining its searchlight over the ghetto. By the time a reporter interviewed them, one of the men had vanished, and there were only three junkies to bear witness to what they saw. The tale faded away, and the gnome was never seen again. The last line of the story made me weep when I wrote it:

Four men were standing around the bonfire warming their hands that night. Only one of them knew he was an angel.

THE STORM became a blizzard half an hour out of town. I had to focus on fighting the wheel, keeping my old Camry on the road. The highways into New Hampshire grew more narrow and winding. Mrs. Feathering, as the old lady had identified herself, had given good directions. Her house outside Keene would have been easy to miss even without the storm, being overgrown with beech and gloomy pines. The huge, scarred trunks provided a wooden fortress around the small, plain box dotted with a few stingy windows—four on the front, two on the sides.

Parking in the shelter of the trees, I walked through the drifts to the front door, which was painted red. The old white clapboards were peeling in blotches, but the door's scarlet coat was shiny and new. Whoever lived inside had rejected the discreet brownish barn red more common to local farms in favor of a color as brazen as a hot shade of lipstick.

Mrs. Feathering must have been lying in wait behind this door, because it flew open after a single knock.

"You're here," she said. "I didn't think you would find the nerve to come. Why are you so young?"

"I don't know," I said, caught off guard. Mrs. Feathering proved to be even older than her quavery voice indicated—and tiny. Standing below her on the stoop, I was still a head taller.

"If you don't know that, how will you figure the rest out?" she said.

Mrs. Feathering's bent frame gave her shoulders a hump. The white hair frizzing over her head didn't quite hide the bald spot on top. Yet her eyes belied her withered body. They showed none of the dullness of age or the china-doll blankness that indicates vacancy of mind. She peered at me sharply, and at that moment, her gaze was disappointed; she didn't bother to disguise it.

"The storm's getting worse. I don't have much time," I said. "Can I come in?"

"*May* I come in," the old lady corrected. But she stepped aside with a slight bow of her humped back.

"My humble abode is yours," she announced with arch courtesy. I brought a cold blast of air in with me, and Mrs. Feathering shivered, drawing the skirt of her faded house dress against the chill. I found myself in a bare hallway with stairs directly in front and a room to either side. This was old New England symmetry, left matching right, room for room, window for window. The old lady gestured to the parlor, which lay left, and I followed.

"Do you live here with your family?" I asked. It was too unnerving to come out with what was really on my mind.

"Oh no, just myself. My husband died twenty years ago. This was his place, inherited from his folks. We used to live in town before that." The old lady, playing along, sounded as bland as I did.

Walking up to the front door, I had already guessed there was no man around. The unraked leaves under the mantle of snow were deep enough to hide a lawn mower. Two shutters hung by a single hinge, and the garage door handle, I could see, was thickly cobwebbed.

"You haven't wandered into anything crazy," said Mrs. Feathering, reading my fears. "Actually, *you're* likely to wind up being the one they call crazy." She laughed, another of her short barks on the edge of harshness.

It took a few more seconds for my eyes to adjust. I sat down on a deep, soft couch covered in bright cotton, not the expected hard Victorian relic. The old lady lowered her frail body slowly down next to me. She wanted to get a closer look, I thought, with her peering eyes. At the other end of the room a fire was going, and a large TV played on mute, tuned to CNN.

"I just need to know why I'm here," I said.

"To get a charmed life. Or perhaps I should say to get back a charmed life. It's very simple. I am instructed to tell you everything," she added.

"Who instructed you?" I was feeling a new kind of uneasiness at the thought that someone else was involved.

"It doesn't matter. I was put on to you years ago, of course. You understand that by now, don't you?" When I didn't reply, Mrs. Feathering grew impatient. "Young man, we won't get anywhere by playing cat and mouse. You found the message, you responded. I told Elena that would prove you were the one. So I was right."

I worked myself up to a one-word reply. "Elena?"

"Yes, yes. All in good time." Without warning Mrs. Feathering reached into a pocket and pulled out some money, a roll of bills wound tightly with a rubber band. She put the wad into my hand before I had a chance to pull away. I eyed the cash and then put it on the coffee table.

"Those are hundred-dollar bills," Mrs. Feathering said, cocking her head like an ancient, gray parrot.

No one gets rich working for a free paper handed out in boxes around Boston. The roll of money represented a lot more than I could expect to earn in six months, to judge by its fatness. Nevertheless, it didn't interest me as much as trying to get Mrs. Feathering to make sense.

"Maybe you saw an article of mine, and that's why you know I'm a writer," I ventured cautiously. "Is that what you're offering me money for, you need some writing done?"

"You can write all you like, but the money isn't a salary. It's a gift, so you won't be distracted," she said.

"Distracted from what?" It was amazing how swiftly the old woman jumped from one illogical point to the next.

"The mystery," she said with complete matter-of-factness. "I mean, you have grasped that much, haven't you? None of this is *normal*." She put a twist on the last word, an upward lilt as if she was teaching vocabulary to a slow six-year-old.

"Excuse me for being blunt," I said, "but mysteries aren't my line, and you can't give me a charmed life. I don't need one." I got to my feet. "I have to get back now," I said, raising my voice to make sure the emphasis sank in.

"Why?" she asked.

"Because there's nothing here, Mrs. Feathering. You know a few things about me—I can't completely explain how. Maybe you did a little research or maybe you fancy yourself a psychic; it's not my concern."

This reasonable explanation sounded pretty shaky, actually, but Mrs. Feathering cut me off. "Wouldn't a psychic ask you to cross her palm with silver? I'm crossing yours."

"I'm sorry, there's nothing you can say."

"But I'm trusting you," she said, as if that answered all objections. "Not just anybody gets to learn about the mystery. Not at all. You are incredibly fortunate. In time you'll realize that fact, but meanwhile—"

I interrupted her. "Meanwhile you think you can bribe me to play along with your queer notions. I don't mean to hurt your feelings, but living alone like this, by yourself, and at your age . . . Well, it's done something."

I spoke with conviction, but halfway through this speech, which was meant to extract me from the house, my voice thickened and blurred. I could barely make out my own words. My next recollection was disconnected.

"It's time that you proved yourself," a distant voice said. "Wake up."

"What?" I sat up feeling confused and disoriented.

I didn't know how I had gotten back down on the couch or how long ago I had checked out.

"You dozed," Mrs. Feathering said. "Only for a minute."

Apparently, however, I had been out longer. The TV was turned off, and the old lady was peering at me from an overstuffed chair by the fire.

"You're ready now," she said.

"Am I?"

Despite having no idea what she meant, I wasn't in a resisting mood anymore. My mind should have been sending up red flags, warning me that paranoid people often talk like Mrs. Feathering. They live in a world of shadowed mysteries that only they understand. Strangely, I felt at ease with her—lazier and more comfortable than I had any right to feel.

"Ready for what?" I asked.

"A test, but not here. We have to go outside." Mrs. Feathering jumped up and grabbed me by the hand. I noticed that she had used the time while I was asleep to throw on her coat, a thick wool astrakhan like the ones men used to wear in old spy movies. She looked like a Russian commissar who'd swallowed a shrinking potion. I found myself being dragged out the door. Snow was still falling but more gently now.

"Where are we going?" I asked.

"I can't tell you. That's the test." Mrs. Feathering kept moving with me in tow.

"Is it far? Tell me that at least."

"Don't ask questions. You need to be calm. It's important."

I intended to play along. I could see only a couple of inches of accumulation on my car as it stood beneath the largest pine tree. But the sight of the Camry reminded me of Boston, and I remembered the treacherous roads and the long drive back.

"I really can't," I said suddenly. "My car's a beater. I don't want to get stuck out here in the dark."

"You mustn't go, not yet!" The old lady's hand closed on me with a surprisingly tight grip.

I could have pulled away. Yet the whole story, as she had foretold on the phone, seemed to want to play itself out, and I let myself be coaxed around the house along a path cut between tall ragged hedges. In the woods that stood at the rear of the house, the gray light faded to black.

"You're not expecting me to go in there," I said.

There was a blinding flash, and I had to cover my eyes. Mrs. Feathering had produced a large flashlight from the depths of her coat. "I can take you a little farther, then you're on your own," she said.

"You're joking. Be reasonable."

Without answering, Mrs. Feathering let go of my hand and plunged on toward the woods, making a shining path for herself. Icy sparkles of snow danced in the flashlight beam.

"I'm not going in there," I called after her.

"You've come this far," she said, turning to face me.

"It's too dark, and the storm makes it dangerous to be out here." This last wasn't true, although the snow was blowing hard enough that Mrs. Feathering's coat had epaulets of powdery white. She turned back and gazed into the brooding firs and pines.

"Lost," she mumbled, looking confused and suddenly exhausted. I waded through the foot-high drifts and grabbed her hand.

"Let me take you back inside," I said gently.

"But you need to try, you need to see," mumbled Mrs. Feathering, uttering one last protest. I led her around the house and almost had to lift her across the threshold before she was deposited back in her living room. She sunk into the deep, soft cushions of her sofa. The fire had died down to coals, and the room looked eerie in their glow, as if I had wandered into the Black Forest with its carved owls on the mantel and gothic shadows. In her black coat with melting snow dripping off it, Mrs. Feathering could have been a beast from the forest.

"Are you sure you're okay by yourself?" I asked.

"I knew you were useless," she whispered. "I shouldn't have told you a thing."

Mrs. Feathering closed her eyes and settled back, ready to hibernate. For a moment her voice regained its focus. "Once I could have made you forget everything you heard here. Now all I can do is make you doze. Once—"

By the time I let myself out into the night, she was already asleep.

I COLLAPSED into bed so tired I could barely pull off my shoes. The drive home was brutal. The bald tires on the Camry kept stalling on hills and fishtailing around sharp curves. None of the country roads were lit, and the snow crews had gone to bed. But exhaustion doesn't always buy oblivion. In the middle of a dead man's sleep, I woke up with a start. At first I thought street noise had startled me, but the bedroom was quiet except for a faint rustling. In the thick dark, I saw that someone else was in the room.

She stood in the far corner by the door wearing a heavy coat, as if dressed for the blizzard. It was too dim for me to see colors. I made out her body, which was tall and willowy, and long black hair surrounding a pale face.

"Do you see me?" she said, coming closer. I lay still. My body hadn't reacted with alarm at the intruder—I knew this was a dream. If I tried hard enough, I would feel my closed eyelids and hear my slow breathing. The woman came closer, her dark coat brushing the sheets. My skin felt cool even though I was under the covers. These sensations didn't mean anything. Dreams are about emotion, and suddenly I felt a powerful one. Gratitude. *I was grateful to be found.*

A place over my breastbone was throbbing now. I opened my mouth to say, "Tell me your name." Nothing came out.

The next thing I knew it was morning, and I was squinting at the ceiling. The whole room was bright with reflected snow. It took a moment to remember the woman, and although I hadn't been startled when she had appeared, my impulse was to jump out of bed now and try all the locks to make sure no one had broken in. I wasn't grateful anymore. I rolled heavily out of bed. When I opened the blinds I saw a city made over by the storm. The jutting corners of the rooftops in the South End had soft shoulders of snow. The traffic down below on Mass. Ave. didn't roar past but glided along with a cushiony whoosh.

Everything I've just told you was coming back in one tangled ball. I couldn't unravel it, and for some reason I didn't want to. The only thing I wanted just then was to find my car keys, which had walked off somewhere between the front door and the bedroom. I grabbed up my parka from the floor and reached into the pockets. I felt something, but it wasn't a set of keys.

A roll of hundred-dollar bills. Mrs. Feathering wasn't giving up, apparently. She had managed to slip the money in while I was dozing in the warm cave of her living room. I stared at the roll and riffled the edges of the crisp new bills. What now?

If I was anxious to confront her, I had a pretext. Not that I needed more confrontations, but a glaring fact poked through the haze of my mind. I hadn't asked her about the ad. It was a blatant oversight—the one thing that had gotten me up there I'd let slip past me. Clearly Mrs. Feathering had been luring me and no one else. But why had she woven this subtle, pointless web? Unless it merely set the stage for a disturbing dream. Was that possible?

My speculations were interrupted by the jangle of the phone. I got it and heard the voice of my sister Linny, off and running without a hello.

"Do you know how to deep-fry a turkey?"

"No, it sounds dangerous," I said, shaken from my reverie and reminded that Thanksgiving was three days away. My sister lives on the shore with her husband and two children. Her religion is all things family.

Linny said, "I think it sounds volcanic. But Josh is on the rampage. He wants to try it, and now he's got this massive kettle out in the garage and enough olive oil to float a boat. I sent him out to buy a fire extinguisher. I mean, for God's sake, we have children we want to see grow up."

Over the years, my older sister and I remained close, both going to college and settling up north. She knit our two lives together with a stream of phone calls every week, a gossipy ritual that I enjoyed. Right now, however, I wasn't really listening. My eye remained fixed on the roll of money sitting on top of my dresser.

It would be easier to resist temptation if I told somebody.

When Linny paused for breath I said, "I saw this queer thing in the paper yesterday. It was about two lovers meeting in secret."

"In the *Globe?*"

"Yeah." In the background I could hear kitchen sounds. I imagined Linny propelling herself around her big kitchen with the new granite countertops and stainless steel appliances.

"How secret could it be if it was announced in the paper?" Linny asked. "Hold on a second."

The phone went dead for a moment. I walked over to the dresser and fingered the money.

"Sorry," Linny said when she came back. "Little Josh was screaming about his soccer ball. Wait till you have kids. Oh, that reminds me. Can you bring a bottle of red when you come for Thanksgiving? And there's room for an interesting girl if you haven't driven them all away. Any new candidates I should know about in advance?"

It seemed strange that she would totally forget what we'd been talking about. I said I would bring the red wine though probably not the girl. Linny seemed satisfied and hung up. Throwing on some clothes, I headed out to go to the post office, where I would shove Mrs. Feathering's wad of bills into a virtuous overnight packet and walk away. I stopped off for coffee first, then I bought a falafel from the Syrian vendor in front of the T stop. Not long after, I wasn't too surprised when I found myself in my car throwing it into gear.

BECAUSE I KNEW the way now, I returned to the small house behind its fortress of trees much faster than before. I got out and walked up to the front door. I gave three knocks, one much louder than the rest. No answer.

"Come on," I muttered.

I waited for a count of ten and tried again. Standing under the eaves was much colder than out in the sun. I stamped my boots and turned away, but instead of getting back into my car, I went around the corner of the house. I could see the blurry imprint of the tracks that Mrs. Feathering and I had made the evening before. They led through the opening in the tall hedge and ended at the border of the woods.

I followed this trail and kept going. The woods quickly closed in on me, but the mid-afternoon light was strong and clear. I could see my way easily, and after five minutes of tramping, I came upon a small clearing.

Instinctively I knew that this was where Mrs. Feathering had wanted to bring me. In spring the open circle would turn into a grassy meadow with nodding yellow jonquils—or would it be a seeping bog rife with pitcher plants and tiny pink wild orchids? At that moment, however, it was a flat white plane crisscrossed with rabbit tracks. I noticed a peculiar hummock in the middle of the glade. I walked over and kicked it. A flurry of loose snow came up, and with it a layer of soggy leaves. I kicked again. Now a limb could be seen half sticking up—but not a tree limb.

An arm. It would have been disturbing except that the arm was gracefully curved and made of marble.

"Who are you?" I murmured.

I knelt and wiped more snow and leaves away. A shoulder emerged, then a naked torso. It was the statue of a youth. The head was more buried than the rest in the sticky mud. I grunted, trying to heave it out and get a better look.

"You'd think anyone could find it, wouldn't you? It wasn't that hard to do."

The voice behind me was a woman's, but it didn't belong to Mrs. Feathering. I kept tugging at the buried statue without turning around.

"No, it wasn't that tough. And I think I've gotten to the bottom of our mystery," I said.

The statue was life size, a lot more than I could lift. I gave up for the moment and wheeled around. Facing me from the edge of the clearing was a young woman. She was tall and willowy, and she wore a black coat that dragged in the snow.

"Why are you looking at me like that?" she said.

Because you came to my room last night. I couldn't say anything that improbable. But the throbbing place over my breastbone came alive again. My impulse was to fight for control.

"Is the old lady your grandmother? She wanted me to find this for her," I said. The young woman threw back the long black hair around her pale face. There was no mistaking that I'd dreamed about her. To keep from saying too much, I knelt back down and began to rock the statue harder to see how stuck it was in the half-frozen muck. "If this is what Mrs. Feathering lost, she can stop worrying," I said.

I glanced at the young woman again and noticed that she was out of breath. The crimson smudges on her cheeks grew deeper. She must have spied me from the upper floor of the house and come running.

"You need some help," she asked. Before I could refuse the offer, she strode quickly across the glade on her long legs and crouched down in the snow opposite me.

"Push when I say so," she said. The young woman gave the signal, and we rocked the statue as hard as we could. At first the added effort seemed to make no difference. Then, all at once, there was a popping sound as the mud released the marble boy.

"Let go," I ordered. With a swiveling motion I twisted the figure onto harder ground. After that, it was relatively simple to hoist it back to standing position.

"Lovely," the young woman murmured, standing back to admire.

"I wonder how it got buried like this," I said, wiping my dirty hands in the snow. "It's too heavy for a storm to blow over. Maybe the ground shifted when heavy rains came in."

The young woman erupted in a peal of laughter. Either she was easily impressed or I was making an idiot of myself. I didn't spend time wondering what Mrs. Feathering had said about me. "If I had to guess, you must be Elena," I said.

The young woman gave a quick tiny smile of acknowledgment. "I'm a little amazed you found it," she said, seeming genuinely surprised. There was an awkward pause while we took each other's measure. I remembered why I had come.

"Here." I pulled the wad of money from my parka. "She gave me this as some sort of retainer, I guess. Tell her I still can't accept, okay?"

Elena didn't reach out to take the roll from my hand. Her whole attention had returned to the statue. Despite its wobbly stance and the considerable residue of dirt lining every crevice, it had presence.

"Amor," she murmured dreamily.

"What do you mean?" I asked.

"It's Latin. In Greek they called him Eros. But by any other name, right?"

I smiled at her. As baffled as I was to find a woman I'd met in my dreams, I wasn't that bothered. In fact, I felt pretty good all around.

"Amor," I repeated, savoring the mystique of those syllables, centuries after they had first been spoken. I picked up a chunk of crusted snow and tried to clean one of the bigger areas of marble, but the muck was glued on. There was no telling how long the earth had had the statue in its grip.

"You may have to get somebody professional out here," I said, giving up. My hands were scraped raw, and several knuckles were bloody. I hadn't noticed until then how much they hurt. Suddenly Elena began laughing again, only this time I knew it was aimed at me.

"I'm sorry," she said. "But you have all these explanations for things, and they sound so crazy."

"Your grandmother didn't want me to find this statue?" I asked, keeping my voice even. Before, I had concentrated on digging up the marble boy because I was afraid Elena would strike some powerful emotion in me, as she had in my dream. Now I was just irritated.

"Dolly's not my grandmother," she said, still amused by me. "You were lying naked in bed, and I talked to you from some place you can't imagine, and now you act like this is all normal? Wouldn't you laugh?"

"You knew you were in my room?" I stammered.

"Try and put this together. Dolly didn't lose this statue. It's just a symbol. Of you. You're the one who's buried and needs to be pulled out."

"No," I said. "You're just doing a number on me. Both of you."

"We're not." Elena was watching me carefully, no longer amused.

"Prove it."

"I can, you know." She kept me in her gaze. "Please try and hear me. You came, and against all odds you succeeded. This statue is love, and love is where you came from. Everything you see here is you and only you."

Her words defied common sense, but part of me didn't care. It was the part that had been on a secret mission, so secret I didn't know about it myself. This part wanted me to stand there and listen and get everything the girl was saying. Yet the rest of my mind wouldn't cooperate.

I heard my voice stumble. "You aren't allowed to do this to me." I spoke each word evenly, with a space in between, but a swirling, gray confusion was swallowing me up.

"You're getting upset." Elena took my face between her hands. They felt clammy from the sweat that was pouring from me. "You need to hold on."

"No," I said, not because I didn't want to. It wasn't possible to hold on. Someone had turned me loose too soon. In some dim remote recess of my brain, a kind of jubilation wanted to erupt, but it couldn't get past the swirling, gray confusion. Elena kept watching me. I don't know what kind of reaction she thought her words would produce. Why would she cook up a plot with some old lady to strip my gears?

"This statue isn't me. *I'm* me," I babbled.

When you're making that kind of sense, something big is about to happen. I clutched at the fog, praying that the sound rolling in wasn't a train.

"I'm sorry," said Elena, her mouth close to my ear. "It's time to jump."

I backed away. My body was flaming with heat, and I tore open my parka to let in some cold. The gray fog got brighter until I was blinded and stumbling through the snow. Then I heard it. Some crazy loon was doing a wild dance, stomping and kicking up cold powder in my face. His arms were flailing, and I could hear him shout so close and loud he could have been me.

"Whoo-ee!"

The loon began to cavort. His berserk rapture was as irresistible as an attack of nausea or stabbing pain, except that it flung me to the opposite of everything sick or painful.

You want this to be me? Is that what you want?

I joined the berserk rapture, and the instant I did, the loon jumped inside me or became me. I don't know exactly what he did.

"Whoo-ee, whoo-ee!" My throat emitted the ridiculous cry, and a shower of golden sparkles filled my head. Something had squeezed me so hard that my cells burst with euphoria like a warm, split peach. Then the gold sparkles cleared, like a parting veil, and I saw where I was.

The glade was green and bright with life. A warm breeze touched my cheek. My hand reached up to feel a branch, and instead of touching rough, bare wood asleep for the winter, I felt limber, sappy greenness. My fingers brushed against a blossom, and as I swivelled my gaze, all the trees were clothed in a haze of new buds.

I tried to find Elena with my eyes, but she was nowhere. Then just as quickly the experience turned. My mind could tell that I was about to dance over the edge, and if I went there, I could only come back at my peril. I began grabbing at the air for support, my lungs felt heavy, suffocated. With uncanny swiftness I plunged from joy into terrifying fear. Panic told me an unbearable truth—I would never be in control again.

"JESS, COME BACK. It's okay."

The voice, at first blurry and distant, turned into Elena's. I took a single sharp intake of breath. My elbow twitched in spasm, hitting something hard. I gradually found myself coming to, and as this happened, new facts dawned. I wasn't in the glade; I wasn't outdoors. I was lying on my back on the floor of a small, warm kitchen. My parka and shirt had been torn open (although, thankfully, not my pants. I confirmed this with a startled rush of the hands). My head had not actually exploded—in fact, except for a slight swimminess, I felt normal and awake, awake enough to hear Elena and Dolly giggling.

"I told you," Dolly said. "He didn't break, he just bounced."

My sight was clear enough to see that the two women were seated at an old farm table on country chairs, and with a lack of concern I found absurdly humiliating, they were sipping mint tea. I struggled to sit up, even though my limbs were rubbery and weak.

"How did you drag me inside?" I mumbled.

My question occasioned another round of giggles.

"Stop that," I said irritably. I was on my feet now, shaking snow and dead leaves from my parka. I wobbled into one of the remaining two chairs at the table.

"Don't be offended," Elena said. "We're happy for you."

"I'm thrilled," I growled. Dolly, who wore a long calico house dress of antique vintage, held out the teapot.

I shook my head. "Gin," I croaked. "If you have it."

"Coming right up." The old lady got on a stool and began to rummage around the top shelves of her glass-fronted cupboards. They were in easy reach of my arms, but I let her continue. Elena started to speak, but I cut her short.

"Don't tell me how lucky I am," I warned.

Dolly came down from the highest cupboard with an unlabeled bottle; it had half an inch of clear liquid at the bottom.

"Go ahead," she urged as I stared balefully at the liquid. "It's good."

I took off the cap and upended the bottle without so much as sniffing it. As long as I had ignored my better judgment this far, what worse could happen? The liquid, which didn't remotely taste like gin, went down with a silky burn in the throat. The alcohol instantly made my head buzz, and for a second I thought I would be dizzy again or even vomit. But the sensations passed, and I felt better. Everything else that had been cut loose was reattached. Anarchy was over.

"So just how lucky should I be feeling?" I asked.

Both women were still fairly beaming. Eerie as this was, the fact that they hadn't satisfied my question about how I got inside—or given me a straight answer to anything—made me feel exhausted.

"It could have been much worse," Elena mused. "You could have wandered into the woods for days. You could have mistaken toadstools for strawberries or tree stumps for gargoyles. It would have been smarter, really, to let Dolly lead you when she offered to."

"So it could have been worse, but I still didn't pass your test. Is that what you're saying?" I asked. "I got a toe through the door, and then I blacked out. Where was I supposed to go? Tell me."

"Nowhere in particular," said Dolly. "There are thousands of doors. You just have to perceive them, and when you go through one, you find more images and more doors."

I waved my hand around the room. "This is just an image?" Both women nodded. "So you're figments of my imagination?"

"No," Elena said. "An image isn't pretend. It isn't fake. It's the way you've chosen to see the world. Right now you're choosing this room."

"What about out there?" I pointed toward the woods. "Don't tell me I changed all that."

"Why not? When you're having a dream, would you claim that you can envision a mouse but not an elephant? Do all your dreams have to take place inside a house but not outdoors?"

"That's different."

"Usually," Elena agreed. "So you needed a little nudge from us." This remark must have been another nudge, because for a second I could feel trapped elation trying to surface again. It quickly flickered out.

"What makes it feel so real?" I asked.

"It *was* real. You stepped for a moment into the subtle world," Elena said.

Dolly chimed in. "We didn't lead you into an illusion. Dear me, the places you came from, the things you've trusted all your life, the people you've invested in—*those* are the illusions. Oh yes."

I felt my face grow hot again from the mysterious liquor. I said, "Do I have to agree with this? Is that part of the spell?"

The two women exchanged a look. "What do you mean?" Elena asked.

"I don't know, I'm not even sure I'm allowed to mean anything. The two of you are like witches tossing lightning bolts back and forth over my head." Dolly raised her hands to protest, but I cut her off. "Maybe you can blow my mind," I said, "but that doesn't make this house the real world. Nothing like. I've stepped into your private weirdness. Somebody told me I would. Actually, it was one of my illusionary friends, as you'd call her." I gave a rude laugh, no longer caring about being polite. These women had gotten into my brain and burned some circuits for my own good, but that didn't mean I had to like it. I lurched to my feet.

"You know your stuff, I'll give you that," I said, raising my voice. "You found out about my past, you crept like mischievous imps into my dreams. That's the same as stealing, but you glossed over that part pretty fast," I stopped before my anger got the better of me. The kitchen was beginning to suffocate me; it was all I could do not to bolt from the room. When Dolly saw this, she shot a glance at Elena; I couldn't tell if it was distress or confusion.

"Please stay. We don't want you to feel this way," Elena said, sounding chastened.

"Why should I? To keep being your guinea pig?"

"Guinea pigs are rather attractive creatures," said Dolly wistfully.

I turned on her. "What?" I shouted.

"I don't think that's the right approach at this moment," Elena cautioned.

"Shut up, both of you!" I looked down to see that I was still gripping the neck of the liquor bottle in my fist. The row of white knuckles looked like they were on someone else's hand. I felt dizzy again.

"He must be in shock," Dolly said quietly.

"Why won't you shut up?" I screamed. Wherever this rage was coming from, it didn't care who stood in its way, including me.

I went stiff, bracing for their next move. Which proved to be quite unexpected. They didn't cast an enchanted cobweb over me or stick me with charmed nettles. All the two women did was get up and leave the room. As she passed me, Elena took the bottle from my hand, which willingly released it. She lifted the bottle slowly and then with a quick fling smashed it on the stone floor. Glass flew everywhere, but before it had settled, she jumped up and down with both feet, two stomps that reduced some bigger pieces to dust.

"Good?" she asked when she was done.

"Yeah." I spat the word out with conviction.

"There's lots of china in the other room, too, once you get finished here." Elena was staring straight into my eyes.

I didn't go on a rampage. Not that I wasn't tempted. After the two of them left, I had the kitchen to myself, the feeble light of a November twilight coloring the walls orange. *Damn it,* I thought. I was caught between sobbing and screaming. Enchantment overload will tend to do that.

My fingers fumbled to button my shirt back up. I tramped outside. The crunch of the freezing snow crust was reassuring under my boots. I scooped up a handful of unsoiled snow from under the top crust and wiped my face. I gazed around and saw jumbled tracks leading through the hedge. I had come and gone, and so had others—there was no denying it.

I turned around and peered up at the house. Its stingy windows were shrinking in the dusk. Two days ago, I knew who I was, but I'd missed two things, and they were now the only important things. I had always been alone, and I had always trusted, against the odds, that my aloneness wasn't forever.

The biting cold air cleared my mind, and I knew that the women inside the house were not responsible for how I felt. They weren't toying with me. Something else was.

I stuck my hands in my pockets, and when I felt the roll of hundred-dollar bills, I couldn't help myself. I began to laugh out loud. They weren't letting me go. Who was I fooling? My only hope was that the imps tramping through my mind weren't mischievous after all. I took the money out and with a strong sidearm pitch hurled it into the woods. I could follow its arc for a second before it became a speck disappearing into the pines. The act felt good, and I laughed out loud again.

I just prayed that my newfound courage lasted long enough to walk the ten feet leading back into the house. For it was now the house of my yearning.

THE KITCHEN WAS EMPTY and dark when I went back inside. I smelled something good—dinner on the fire. But there was no cook and no fire. I walked over to the rough plank table and looked down. A place was set for one, and on the plate was a half roast chicken, brussels sprouts, and potatoes with gravy. The meal was meant for me, even though there was no possible way Elena or Dolly could have prepared it the brief time I'd been gone.

I didn't care. All my body knew was that too much exertion and the alcohol had made it very hungry.

"Go ahead. Don't wait for me."

I turned to see Elena leaning against the doorway to the front of the house. In the dimness, I could make out only a willowy shadow. The last rays of the sun were trapped in the gloomy pines out back. "I'm not hungry, but I'll watch while you eat," she said, coming closer.

"How did this food get here?" I asked.

"It's called reheating. How did you think it got here?" Then she caught on and looked amused. "Your brain keeps looking for a magic show."

"Nothing less," I smiled. I sat down, straddling one of the country chairs. "It's going to take a while for me to adapt." It seemed understood between us that I was staying. I asked about Dolly.

"I put her to bed," Elena said. "This has been a lot of excitement for one day." She sat down opposite me with her back to the window. Night hadn't completely fallen, and against the sapphire sky she turned back into a silhouette. She watched me work on the chicken, tearing it in half and eating with my hands. I said, "What's happening? Tell me in simple words, the kind that can be understood by the easily duped."

Elena gave a faint smile. "Why do you think you came here?" she asked.

"You know why. Some tempting words in the newspaper."

"But the main word was *love*. What does that mean to you?" I cringed inside, and she noticed. "I'm not trying to pry. Love makes the world possible. It is the essence of *what is*."

She put an inflection into the last two words that I didn't understand, but I waited to ask her about it. "There are a lot of things that exist without love," I said.

"Do you really think so?"

"I don't just think so. There is evil and hatred. There's all the things born from them—war, crime, poverty—" I stopped. Elena seemed to be taking in what I was saying as something new. "What's making you look so surprised?" I said.

"I'm not surprised. I'm trying to see something in you." All right. I waited for her to explain. "Everything you say has to come from some level of the mind. So where does evil come from? Where does hatred come from?"

"They don't just come from my mind," I said. "They exist."

"No," said Elena. "They aren't part of *what is*. I could show you a level in your mind where evil has no reality at all. That level creates its own world. If you entered such a world, everything that isn't love would be gone."

I was speaking to someone whom I'd called a witch two minutes before. "You can't be that naive," I said. "If I wish evil away in my mind, it won't stop existing. I'll still be in this world, and the bad stuff will be waiting around the corner."

Don't take me to court on this, but I thought I had a perfect argument. No, better than an argument. I had *what is* on my side. If she wanted to use that term, the existence of bad stuff belongs to *what is*, or nothing does.

Instead of replying, Elena apparently made a decision. With a quick gesture she placed her hand over my wrist and held it there. At first I thought she wanted to comfort me or to express that she understood my confusion.

Her gesture wasn't meant to comfort, though. "I'm going to let you into the kitchen," Elena said softly.

"We are in the kitchen."

"But you haven't seen how the cooks work," she said. "Close your eyes and follow my voice. Ready?"

I suddenly realized that despite her hesitancy, Elena had been building up to this moment all along. "Ready," I said.

"I'm going to show you something that I had to learn myself," Elena began.

"Who taught you?"

"Don't ask questions right now, just listen. We're going on a journey." Elena lowered her voice and started to paint a picture. "I want you to imagine yourself as someone else, someone far removed from your present life. It's long ago, and you're a young peasant girl working in the fields. The work is hard, but you're happy and secure. You've never left your village in your entire life. For you, the center of existence is the old church, the market, and all the houses that seem to be a permanent part of the world. You can't even imagine this village had to be built. It has stood here since the beginning of time. Are you tuning in to that?"

I nodded, feeling lulled by the softness of her touch on my hand.

Elena went on. "You are in the fields, bent over putting fresh seedlings in rows. The sun is warm on your back, and you begin to hum a song your mother taught you, a song taught to her when she was your age. Is the image still steady in your mind?"

I nodded.

"Don't be tense," Elena said. "You don't have to do anything. Leave it all up to me."

"Okay."

She gave my wrist a harder squeeze, and instantly the mental picture became twice as sharp and clear. I saw, as if studying a photograph, that the peasant girl was very young, with olive skin and dark eyes. I pulled back.

"Hold on, don't say anything," Elena warned. "Feel how this girl feels. Her way of life seems immortal. Always and forever there have been green fields and distant hills, orchards and vines. As far back as she can think or dream, her people have been given this gentle home by God.

"She doesn't think about whether God is real. She just accepts; she receives what is given. Can you touch that place inside her?"

I hesitated, expecting my lifetime of religious doubt to raise a protest, but I couldn't find any resistance to what Elena was doing.

"You're ready to really *be* her. There is no doubt in your heart now," said Elena. "It's you who kneels to pray every night. You are gazing at the face of the Blessed Virgin. Tell me what you want her to know."

I was quiet for a moment, then I said, "You're with me, Mother. No one understands you the way I do." I would have been shocked to say these words, except that the peasant girl wanted to, and because she meant them, so did I. Elena didn't give me time to analyze.

"You're getting uncomfortable because you and she are too close, I know that," Elena said. "But you must let her merge with you. Nothing bad will happen."

I felt a surge of anxiety, because the girl had become much more than a mental picture. Her emotions were seeping into me like hidden water finding its way through secret passages.

"This girl is just a symbol," said Elena softly. "Behind the picture is an impulse coming directly from your soul."

I gave a sharp sudden exhale. I had no idea that I'd been holding my breath or that what was happening would be so intense.

"Now we are at the last step," said Elena. "Here."

She did nothing but say this one syllable, yet I felt a change. The girl who had been seeping into my being was now completely merged. And all at once I knew why.

"There's a gift for you. Feel her innocence," Elena said softly. "Do you want it?"

The gift was passed before I could reply, in a single intimate breath the girl infused in me. My body accepted the breath. I felt my arms become slim and soft; my chest ached with the sprouting buds of breasts.

Elena's voice kept guiding me. "Innocence is only one aspect of your soul. But it is the most precious, because innocence allows you to receive everything else. Without innocence, you can't feel fully loved. This girl is certain that she is loved, by God and by all that God created around her. When you're ready, tell me about being loved that way. Let her speak."

But I couldn't; I was losing her. The sunlit field had faded out, and I had nothing but my own blank mind. Elena urged me with a strange gesture, lightly tapping the top of my head. All at once the peasant girl returned, only this time she was inside a warm, smoky room with rough, plastered walls.

Before I could adjust to this jump, she said, "I'm by a fire, and it's winter. There are warm flagstones under me, and I've been staring into the flames, watching them make patterns. Without knowing it, I fall asleep. Now someone is picking me up, I feel myself being carried, and from his strong arms I know it's my father. He's always been there to protect me. I worship him, but we don't talk about that. He puts me in my bed, and before I feel him kiss me, I'm asleep again."

I knew with certainty that I had never experienced what she was describing. Yet that didn't matter. Some part of my being craved this primal scene of safety and belonging, craved it so much that I rushed into it willingly, not caring if my own identity got blotted out. I didn't really know where I was, yet a tide of desire shoved me forward with ungoverned force.

"Ow!"

Without warning Elena had slapped me hard in the face. My eyes flew open. Being startled, I couldn't find myself for a few seconds, but that was enough. I was in the room described by the girl. Before me was the dying fire in the hearth, the flagstone floor pressing roughly into my skin—*her* skin. Then I heard the approaching steps of the father and some words in a language I couldn't recognize. Was it medieval Italian? But by then there was no room left for me; I came back to the kitchen with Elena, shifting as smoothly as in a slide show.

"Did it happen?" she asked.

I nodded dumbly. I felt myself trembling and emitting quick, ragged gasps. "Incredible," I muttered. I jumped up and started pacing.

"You might want to lie down or drink a glass of water," Elena warned.

"No, no, I'm fine." My voice sounded more excited and rapid-fire than I expected.

"Hold on," Elena said—the same words, I remembered, that she'd used when I had flipped out in the glade.

"I'm not going to freak," I said, anxious for her to believe me.

"Okay." Elena found the last brussels sprout on the plate and nibbled at it. "You're not flapping your wings and shouting '*Whoo-ee.*' Not that I'd stop you."

I would have accepted the invitation to laugh at myself, except that a second wave of energy was sweeping over me. This one wasn't so good. It had a paranoid flavor mixed with mania.

"Oh man," I said. "Man oh man." I grabbed hold of the galvanized iron sink to steady myself. "Whatever you do, it has some kick later."

"How long did you actually stay where I guided you?" Elena asked, apparently not knowing everything. This came as a minor relief to me.

"I was there for three or four seconds, maybe."

She looked pleased. "That's really very good. You don't realize it now, but I was showing you how everything is made. And you are the maker, always. Nothing exists without you."

"Me? What about you?"

"Nothing could exist without me, either."

"So except for you and me, none of this would be here at all?"

"And Dolly and everyone else. We're all the infinite makers of an infinite world. You wouldn't think it could work that way, but I guess there's enough infinity to go around."

It was too much. In psychology they teach that the uncanny feelings—those that seem to come from outside yourself—include awe, dread, horror, worship, and the premonition of things to come. Every one of those feelings was ganging up on me.

"Try and let it sink in," Elena urged. "What you have been accepting as normal all your life is not. You're afraid right now."

"I'm not," I protested.

"Don't defend your courage. You've been through something that's going to change your life completely." Elena hesitated, drawing a deep breath as if to make sure she wanted to say what she was about to say.

"This house and this piece of ground are sacred. The fact that you made it here and passed the test is nothing short of incredible. You think we surprised you? That's nothing compared to how much you surprised us."

I could see Elena's eyes change. Since I'd met her, they had been deep pools of brown that reflected nothing back. No matter how amazed, enraged, or manic I had been, she continued to regard me with the same level gaze. But now her eyes looked, for just a moment, lost and bewildered. The change ended quickly, but her loss of composure unnerved me.

"I'm an intruder," I mumbled. "I came over the wall, and nobody has done that for a long time."

She didn't deny it. "We had safety before you came. But you reached us, and if that can happen, others will soon be able to do the same." Elena smiled wryly, the smile of an aristocrat forced to open the doors to people with two-dollar tickets and baby carriages rolling over the antique oriental carpets.

I wondered how she could be so disturbed when it was she and Dolly who had led me there.

"It wasn't my idea," she said, reading my question. "Dolly wanted to prove that we weren't meant to be so hidden."

"No one's going to hurt you," I said impulsively.

"You think you're here to protect us? Invaders don't have a history of doing that." Elena laughed with an unmistakable note of derision.

I felt my face grow warm. "If you don't need protection, then you must want something from me."

"We discussed it. Maybe the world has changed its mind. That could be it, couldn't it? You could be a sign."

"You think the world's set against you?"

Elena raised her eyebrows. "Look at your own reaction." She flailed her arms in imitation of my crazed dance in the glade. "It's taken our full attention to keep you from jumping out of your skin. But that's not really it. We're masters of escape. Long ago we saw how unwelcome we were. The average mind would fear us, and being unable to face that fear, it would soon hate us."

"How do you escape?" I asked.

"We have ways. Maybe you'll see."

"When?" I said.

Elena didn't satisfy my curiosity. She began clearing the table and washing dishes in the galvanized sink.

"I'm fascinated—you can see that," I said. "After what you showed me tonight, my deepest wish is that you will show me everything."

"I could show you everything in thirty minutes," Elena said, flashing a grin. "But it would take thirty men to hold you down."

I helped her finish cleaning up. Elena brought down some linens and made up the couch in the living room. As she was damping the fire, I said, "When I called on the phone and wasn't sure about coming here, Dolly told me that the story wants to play itself out."

"She told you that?" Elena's eyes turned inward. "She told me that I would leave with you. We'll be going out there." Elena pointed out the window, and although her finger indicated the general direction of Boston, what was outside at that moment was night's black emptiness. Perhaps she meant both.

She had one last thing to tell me. "Dolly is more than you think she is. She's the last wise woman."

"And what does that make you?" I asked.

Elena gave no reply, slipping away quickly. I heard her stepping lightly as she went upstairs.

I slipped in between sheets that smelled of spiced must and lavender. Were they part of Dolly's marriage dowry, stuck into a cedar chest a thousand years ago? I watched flame goblins dancing in the dying coals. Then my body, more exhausted than I could remember, banished all questions and sought a few hours of blissful unconsciousness.

I WOKE UP early after a dreamless sleep. No one had come to visit me during the night. The first thing I felt was the cold dampness that had leaked through the old house's loose joints. The first thing I saw was a bomb going off. It erupted in flame and smoke, all of it silent.

"Dolly?" I said. She was sitting across the room watching TV. "Do you always look at wars?"

I sat up and wrapped a sheet around myself. She had CNN on mute, so the bombs that exploded, like the jets and helicopters, were eerily noiseless.

"I have my routine," Dolly said.

"I can think of nicer routines."

"So can I. Are you leaving right away?"

"Is that what Elena told you?"

"She told me that you think we're witches, so we'd better get you back home before you run away on your own. Want some gingerbread?" Dolly laughed, sounding very cheery. Her hair was combed, and she was wearing rouge on her cheeks, as if she was ready for a big day or a party. There was no hint that she was the wisest woman in the world.

"I'm not the wisest woman in the world," Dolly said amiably. "I'm the last wise woman."

"I didn't know there was a difference." I stretched my arms and began yawning. Somehow it didn't bother me anymore when she read my mind. It was more economical, really. I felt invigorated. Over Dolly's shoulder, I could spy a narrow shaft of sunlight coming in from the bright outdoors. I'd never seen the interior when the sun was out. Now that I did, the living room didn't look like a cave but a cheerful nest. Bits of blue and white Japanese pottery were set here and there. The walls were hung with flower prints and landscapes. It was hard to find anything that wasn't buoyant, despite Dolly's habit of tuning in to disasters.

"Let me turn that off," I said. Dolly shook her head. "Why not?" I asked.

"I'm watching and waiting."

"For what? The pictures change, but the world isn't going to."

"I'm waiting for a sign that somebody out there has a clue." Dolly turned her gaze toward me. "You came here without a clue."

It was hard to respond to this without looking sheepish, but she wasn't asking for a response.

"People have a right to choose what they want," she said. "I was put here. God put me in this place in case the parade might wish to come to my door. But it never did, and that's nobody's fault. If you'd told me that I would wind up as the last wise woman, well—"

"How did you get to be the last?" I asked, lowering my voice. Growing solemn didn't please her.

"I'm not an egg, you don't have to coddle me," she snapped. "If

I wanted to, I could have you serenading under my window and baying at the moon."

This brought a smile to Dolly's face, and it wasn't an old lady's smile. "I'm letting you off easy this time," she said mischievously. "It's not as amusing to make young men do their tricks as it once was." She sat up with pride, and for a moment, before she sank down into the puffy cushions again, she looked almost straight and tall. "*I know things,*" she said so defiantly that there was a hiss at the end of her sentence.

This was exactly how an oracle might speak after her devotees had abandoned her and the fires had gone cold in the temple.

"What kind of things do you know?" I asked.

"I know a lot about love," said Dolly. "But now I don't even want to hear the word."

"It makes you too sad?"

"No, sadness was never an option. I've had my time, and it was a beaut." The old lady's face lit up with recollection. "I don't like hearing the word because when people use it, they don't mean *real* love. They only mean a feeling. Love doesn't depend on how you feel."

I didn't hide my surprise. "Love has a lot to do with how you feel."

"Do you feel love right now?" Dolly asked. She waited a second. "I didn't think so. But love is pulling at you right now, like gravity. If you let yourself be pulled and don't hold back, you would be able to touch the subtle world. But you've discovered that already, I suppose."

Dolly hadn't been present when Elena took me places, yet she knew I'd been. I had no doubt of that. I said, "If you can live in another world, a world of love, why not go there?" I pointed to the TV. "You don't have to change all that. You can't."

"The reason I can't is because of you," she said firmly. "You're addicted."

"To what?"

She pointed at the TV. "To this mess. It's horrible. Why do you keep insisting on it?" Dolly's cheerfulness vanished, and she looked supremely irritated.

"If people only loved each other, violence would end?" I asked.

"Yes." Dolly punched the remote, and the room was as quiet as the woods outside. She might have let the argument drop, but I was feeling stubborn.

"Love won't work," I said. "For one thing, people already love each other, and they still do awful things. Human beings are violent animals wishing they were angels."

"Like in your story," Dolly interjected.

"That was fiction, and I wrote it when I was pretty young and didn't know any better," I said. "Now I do know better. The beast in everyone is hiding in the underbrush, waiting. It springs out when it wants to, and then horrible disasters occur. Sometimes the worst things happen to those who stand up and preach love. Which is just my way of saying that you should worry and be careful before going too far."

I didn't know why I was lecturing her. But Dolly wasn't offended.

"I'm not the dreamer," she said. "You are."

"To judge by the last two days, you must be right."

She gave me an astute look. "I mean that you want to escape. You want me to fly you to a better world. That's why you've been arguing so pointlessly about trying any other answer." Dolly shook her head. "Of course you'd prefer Elena, the younger witch, to take you there. Pity we only have vacuum cleaners around here— you don't mind flying on them, do you?"

Could I deny any of this? Every strange and wonderful thing that had happened to me in this house revolved around Elena, who had found me in a dream. "I won't call either of you witches anymore," I said, hoping to placate Dolly.

"I've been on a tear, haven't I?" she said, calming down noticeably. Her voice lost its edge, and she assumed a meekness that made her an old lady again. Dolly lifted herself out of the armchair with both hands. "Bathroom, second floor. I'll tell Elena you're ready."

I let her go and went upstairs. In keeping with the kitchen, the bathroom turned out to be a relic. The ancient tub stood on cracked claw feet, and the porcelain sink was yellow with age. I found a brick of soap sitting on a frayed white towel—you couldn't call anything that size a bar of soap—and took my bath in half an inch of hot water, all that the faucet allowed before it turned cold. There was nothing to shave with, and I had to slip back into my stale clothes. When I crept downstairs I found Elena waiting by the front door.

"The day calls," she announced. She wore a colorful tartan skirt and, considering the cold, an optimistically thin green sweater. There was no overcoat or luggage in sight.

"I got impatient and put everything in the car," she said, opening the door and letting in a gust of cold air.

"I thought I locked the car," I said.

Elena smiled elusively and led the way outside. We tramped through snow that was still fairly deep, but the sun had warmed up enough to melt the car clean. We got in, and I saw why Elena hadn't bothered to bid Dolly good-bye. The old lady was curled up in the backseat, cocooned in a thick wool blanket. She appeared to be asleep.

"Is this really such a good idea?" I said doubtfully.

Elena shushed me with a finger to her lips. Any fantasy I might have about taking her away on my white charger vanished into thin air. Apparently I didn't have a say in who I rescued.

We started to back down the sloped, curving driveway. With my eye on the rearview mirror, I missed Elena's reaction as the house disappeared behind the trees. We reached the road and I turned for Boston. Looking over at her, I could see no sign of regret or apprehension in Elena's face. Dolly didn't care enough about leaving to wake up. But then it was only my suspicion that told me they would never return.

Light snoring was coming from the backseat. I looked over my shoulder and saw beside Dolly two small suitcases and a vanity bag, along with Elena's long black coat.

"That's all you're bringing?" I said.

Elena nodded, and although her expression didn't change, I heard the release of a small sigh. She said. "I looked at the map, and we have only about an hour and a half to travel, right?"

"More or less."

"Good." Elena sat up with her eyes straight ahead. She sat perfectly erect, like the narrow brick houses that march up and down the few remaining hills in Boston. Elena seemed to be the kind of woman who could march up and down hills. I didn't know what else she was capable of.

"What do you really think of me?" I said, breaking the silence after we found the main highway.

"A lot of things," Elena said.

"Come on."

"Well, you're not unappealing."

I gave a wry laugh. "You say that with such excitement."

"I'm mentioning it because it will be useful." Elena looked back at Dolly, who hadn't moved since we left. She was deep enough in sleep that neither of us had to whisper. "You're going to meet women, and sex appeal will be useful."

I remembered Dolly's remark that guinea pigs are rather attractive creatures.

"Is that all you think, that I'll be useful?"

"Perhaps."

Elena didn't like me fishing around, either for compliments or candor. So I let it rest. We drove a while longer without talking. Soon we came to the outskirts of Boston. Elena didn't look expectant or curious. But she had something on her mind.

"When I said that Dolly was the last wise woman," she remarked without preface, "I didn't mean she was like the last whooping crane. She's the last until the next comes along. One link in a chain."

"So there's only one wise woman at a time?" I said.

"We don't know for sure. But Dolly has spent her whole life trying to find another one like her, and she never did."

"How does somebody win the title?"

"It's not a contest," Elena said. "But there is only one at a time. She possesses the vision."

I guess I made it sound like Dolly had gone a few rounds in the ring with a contender. The same image must have come to Elena's mind, because she giggled. "She didn't win it. She was told."

"By the wise woman before her?"

"Yes. I didn't tell you, but Dolly grew up in Boston," Elena said. "When she was a child, they used to walk kids to school in a straight line with one chaperone in front holding up a flag and another in back to keep watch."

"They still do that." I had seen similar processions mornings and afternoons on my run.

Elena nodded. "Dolly's parents were fairly well-to-do, and she was protected more than a girl could stand now. It was meant for her own good, but she was a rebel. Even at five or six she would dawdle on the street, getting out of line to pick up a gum wrapper or stare at corsets in a store window. When the chaperone shooed her back into line with the other girls, Dolly obeyed, but she never stopped looking around.

"One day a scrap of paper fell onto the sidewalk in front of her. No one seemed to notice except Dolly, who looked up to see a woman in the window overhead. The woman pointed at the scrap of paper and then immediately ducked back in. By this time Dolly was already out of step with her group, but she snapped up the paper and shoved it into her pocket to read later. When she got to school, she opened the note, which said, *I bet you can't read this.*

"Dolly had already formed the habit of secrecy; she told no one. But the next morning she made sure that neither chaperone was looking her way as they went by the house. She pulled a folded paper from her pocket and dropped it on the ground beneath the window. On it she'd written, *I bet I can.* She waited anxiously all day, and coming back to the same spot on her way home, the note was gone."

"How old was Dolly?" I asked, finding it easy to imagine everything else about the story.

"Seven or eight, I think. Old enough so that she could read every note that was dropped from the window from then on. There was a note a day. They told a story revealed to her one scrap at a time."

"By the last wise woman," I guessed.

"Right. However, Dolly didn't know that and wouldn't have understood if she had been told. All she knew was that the story was fascinating."

For the rest of the way to Boston, I got the hear the story, which went like this: There once was a mermaid who wandered the streets of Boston dawdling from her group and staring into shop windows. She wasn't looking at bonnets and skirts but rather for her tail, which had been stolen.

The tail, made of shiny green and gold scales, was extremely beautiful. Anyone who set eyes on it would be unable to resist the temptation to steal it. The mermaid couldn't remember who stole hers, only that she had woken up one day without it. Her parents, along with the other mer people, banished her from the sea until she got it back again.

After many tears and much trouble, she found herself having to live the life of a normal girl. No one believed she was a mermaid, the obvious proof, her tail, being missing. But the mermaid knew who she was, so she kept quiet and never stopped looking. One day she was passing by a fishmonger's, and there in the glass case, sitting on ice beside the cod and halibut, was her tail. It had been sold by the fisherman who first stole it, and the fishmonger, realizing its value, had hidden it away. But when no one came to reclaim it, he grew proud and wanted the public to see that he possessed this splendid thing. Elena got this far and then she paused.

I said, "Okay, how did she get the tail back?"

Elena shook her head. "I don't think the story ever found an ending. By the time it got that far, Dolly had caught on. She knew that she was the mermaid, but more than that, she had also figured out that the woman in the window possessed special knowledge. Otherwise, how would she have known to make up such a story that fit one particular girl so well?"

"Most kids think that fairy tales are about them," I pointed out.

"That's true," Elena conceded. "But Dolly ran away one Saturday morning and knocked on the door where the woman in the window lived. She was greeted with open arms. There was hell to pay when Dolly got back home—and a lot of interrogation. She had to be more secretive than ever. In fact, she told me it wasn't possible to return to the last wise woman's house for another five years, except for stolen moments. When she was old enough to break free, Dolly's teacher, who was called Miss Sophia, started to instruct her seriously."

"The way Dolly started instructing you," I said.

"We met in a very different way. I was already grown. She didn't have to drop notes from the sky." A recollection came back that made Elena smile. "I was almost as stubborn as you. I wouldn't believe that it was all about me."

"You think I'm stubborn?"

A voice came from the backseat. "You most certainly are. The two of you make a pair."

"I didn't know you were awake," Elena said, not bothering to turn around. Dolly was sitting up folding her blanket.

"When am I not awake?" she asked cryptically. "Isn't that our turn?"

She pointed at the exit I was about to miss. I swerved right and made the day of the driver next to me. The countryside had already turned to suburbs and in the two-lane roads into four. It took another twenty minutes before we got off near downtown and headed for the South End. In this part of town every house has a past, usually far more elegant than its present. Streets lined with worn brick facades waited for someone to bring them back to life.

"Does it all look strange to you?" I asked. Elena and Dolly hadn't said a thing since the off-ramp. I assumed they were taken aback by what looked normal to me—congested streets, panhandlers, dirty windows, and graffiti.

"It looks like any city, as much as I can remember," Dolly mused. "I don't think I could get to like it again."

Elena was more emphatic. "It can be whatever it wants," she said. "We can change it easily enough."

I found a parking space close to my building. Elena helped Dolly out while I unloaded the luggage. We didn't say much as we walked to my apartment. I didn't really know how they felt, and almost against my will I found my mind drifting back to automatic. I had forgotten to call my sister back about Thanksgiving. An unfinished story on the homeless living in the Fens was lying on my desk at the office. There was e-mail and phone mail and snail mail to open. Had my life really been nothing but this confetti of details showering down day after day?

After I led the way through the lobby and we took the elevator up, I unlocked my apartment and stood aside. Dolly went in first. "I'm sorry the place is a wreck," I said.

"The vibe is nice; it feels like you," Dolly remarked, then she added. "They both need a little work." Hearing someone who looked like she should be sewing a quilt use the word *vibe* caught my fancy. I laughed and gestured for them to go in.

I was watching Elena closely. You can tell a lot from how a person enters your home for the first time. Elena didn't gush or look around curiously or pick up the first thing that caught her eye. She didn't march in to occupy the ground like a homesteader or throw herself on the furniture as if she already lived there. She contented herself with a quick glance and said, "Dolly's right. It's you."

I found that pretty ambiguous, really. I opened a window to let out the mustiness and showed them the bedroom.

"This will be yours. I'll throw a sleeping bag down on the floor in the living room," I said. While I put her luggage on the unmade bed, Elena pulled off her green sweater, revealing a surprisingly skimpy white top, and tied the sweater around her waist.

"Can we start today?" she said, looking out the window. The sky was fair and the icicles were dripping from the eaves.

"Definitely," said Dolly, who was testing the mattress by bouncing on it. She couldn't have liked what she found.

"Start on what? Me or the vibe?" I joked. The question came out casually, which made me slightly proud given the scary prospect of what these two were capable of.

"Neither." Elena faced me with determination in her eyes. "Thank you for inviting us, but we can't stay."

"Is something wrong? You're already here, why not stay?" I said.

"I should have told you not to bring up the bags, but I lost focus for a while." She turned to Dolly. "Let's get you out of here."

Elena was so brusque that I didn't know how to react. Dolly, who didn't seem remotely surprised by this about-face, eased herself up from the bed. It took her a while to cover the short distance to the front door; I trailed slowly behind.

"All right," I said, doing my best to adjust and trying not to jump to conclusions. "I guess this is for the best. Do you know where you're going to stay?"

Nobody answered my question. Elena was muttering to herself in short bursts. "The banks are still open. I'll wait on the real estate agents. Oh, the phone—please find it for me. Portable, and you can wait in the hall. Dolly won't mind keeping you company."

"The hall?" I said. It took me only a moment to fetch the portable phone from where it had been hiding under a pile of clothes. I handed it over and helped Dolly out. Elena followed to shut the door behind us. When we were out in the hallway, Dolly regarded me calmly.

"Why did she do that?" I asked.

"She needs the privacy. We always work alone. And perhaps she's afraid of your karma," Dolly said.

Sore as I was, I wanted to laugh. "Where did you learn that word?"

She shrugged. "One has to keep up." Through the flimsy door panel, I could hear Elena talking on the phone, but the sound faded quickly—Elena had gone into the bedroom. These signs of mistrust rattled me.

"What does she know about my karma?" I said sourly.

"Oh, it's nothing personal," said Dolly. "I'm sure your karma isn't a disaster. At least, I hope not. But we're out in the world now. There are all kinds of vibrations"—she didn't say vibe this time—"and we don't want to attract the wrong ones. Karma means something you attract to yourself, I think."

For someone trying not to jump to conclusions, I suddenly jumped to a big one. They were leaving because of my attraction to Elena. The notion that I wasn't supposed to be attracted didn't sit well. Some people might call Dolly's remark pretty damn rude.

"Some people might call it worse than that," she said amiably.

"It would be a lot easier on me if you didn't step into my mind without being invited," I grumbled. Dolly didn't reply, and we waited for Elena to finish her calls. The hallway was dimly lit with forty-watt bulbs, one of the stingier economies of the building. The jumpiness that had disappeared when I went to Dolly's house returned, and I began to pace the worn-out gray carpet.

"I imagine you'll be staying in a lot nicer place," I said.

"Oh, yes," said Dolly. "I'm sure Elena will inform you in due time."

An ugly suspicion reared its head: I was expendable. I had been useful only up to a point, but this would be good-bye—they had planned from the outset to go about their mysterious work without me. And why not? Dolly was used to solitude and probably demanded it. Elena wasn't interested in me. She was patently secretive. She walked through walls at night and could creep in on you without so much as a by-your-leave.

"She makes Circe look like the Easter bunny," said Dolly. "Oh, I forgot to ask permission to read your mind. Please forgive me. It comes so naturally anymore."

"I bet." Actually, I was glad for the intrusion; my panicky thoughts might begin to dissolve if Dolly distracted me. "Do you read Elena's thoughts?" I asked.

"I don't have to."

"Because you're so close?"

"Something like that. Elena and I meet in the subtle world, and there you don't have to hide your thoughts. It's one of the great advantages—but then, it's also one of the reasons most people stay away."

I figured as long as we were alone, Dolly might say something to quiet my fear that I would never see them again. "Where is the subtle world?" I asked.

"Here," she replied. "It's closer than anything. You're in it all the time, but you don't see."

"And you do?"

"Of course. Ninety percent of being wise is knowing your way around the subtle world."

"Do you see some other place where we're standing?"

"Hm." I didn't get what was so hard about my question, but Dolly was thinking hard. "I don't switch out one place for another. It's not like arranging furniture. But if I had to see different shapes, they would appear. Mostly it's about tone—like knowing the truth about a person no matter how hard they try to lie. A place can also lie. You never know."

There was no doubt that Dolly spoke with complete familiarity about this puzzling realm, but we were still in a shabby hallway with stingy lightbulbs.

"I can draw you a picture," she suggested, sensing my dilemma. "It will give your mind something to hold on to. Now, imagine nothing. Just a blank, open space, stretching in all directions."

"Like outer space?"

Dolly nodded. "Only emptier. This nothing can't be seen; you can't even think about it. But it is alive. It doesn't have to move to prove it's alive. It doesn't have to show any sign at all. Like your mind when you're asleep, this emptiness is ready to wake up. What happens to you when you wake up? You don't have to run through a list of who you are and assemble all the parts of yourself—memories, likes and dislikes, what your name is and where you live. No, when you wake up, who you are is instantly there. Do you understand?"

"I think so. Even though my mind is a blank when I'm asleep, it's actually holding on to everything about me."

Dolly looked pleased. "This nothing I described to you wanted to wake up, and when it did, everything that could possibly exist did exist. All at once and without any time passing. First there was nothing, then there was everything.

"Now, you can see that this kind of instant everything wouldn't be easy to live in. Think of where we're standing. Right now it is a building, but a hundred years ago it might have been a marsh or a hill. Before that it was a volcano or the bottom of the sea. Before that it was dust. So if everything existed at once, we would find ourselves feeling very uncomfortable standing here.

"But this nothing-that-turned-into-everything had an answer: time. To make it easier to live with millions and millions of things, it laid them out in a sequence, and we call it time. This trick was very effective, because not only is it comfortable to go from A to B, but you don't have to think about Z before you get there. Yet as soon as time came into the picture, there was another problem. Forgetting. Time stretches so far that you tend to forget where you've been after a while. Imagine that a person went to all the trouble of building a horse, but a year later the atoms and molecules in that horse forgot what they're doing and started to go back to being random dust and raindrops and air. Very messy.

"So the nothing-that-turned-into-everything needed glue. This glue would hold everything together. It would remember what goes where. And most important, it wouldn't be fooled by this trick called time. It would see the truth, that everything was created all at once and fits together perfectly."

"What was the glue?" I said.

"Love. Love is the glue that keeps things from falling apart. Love makes you feel immortal because you stop being fooled by time. When you love, you suddenly remember *what is.*"

Dolly told her story very simply, but when she finished I felt goose bumps. She had given my mind an awesome picture to hold on to—but I still had a question.

"How does the subtle world fit in?" I said.

She hesitated. "I don't know if I should tell you."

"Why not?"

"Because the subtle world might reveal more than you want to know." Dolly looked genuinely worried, but I was baffled.

"What kind of thing would bother me that much?" I asked.

She sighed. "Well, you don't like me reading your mind. In the subtle world, everybody knows everything. Can you live with that?" She didn't wait for a reply. "Let's say you feel brave and say yes. What about falling in love? Are you ready to give that up?"

"Why would I have to?"

"For the same reason fish have to give up being thirsty. In the subtle world there is only love. You can't fall in love because you never fall out of it."

"I don't understand why you think I'd be afraid of that," I protested. "It's like paradise, isn't it?"

Dolly shook her head. "Your idea of paradise is like one long picnic where everything is luscious. In the subtle world there's no contrast, so being in love doesn't feel luscious. It just is."

I began to feel more sober about this whole thing. "So you're saying I'd have to give up some things that down here seem critical," I said hesitantly. "I mean, feeling that you love somebody keeps people going."

She nodded. "You won't give up anything, but many things will be transformed." She thought for a moment. "Imagine Elena falling in love with you, and imagine Elena having always loved you. Which would you choose?"

"I don't know."

"Are you sure?"

It was amazing how quickly Dolly had gotten to the heart of my predicament. Of course I had been nursing a lot of fantasies around Elena. I told you a few of the paranoid ones—that she might say good-bye and never come back, that she might be a witch and not to be trusted. But there were good fantasies, too, including the possibility that Elena might fall for me. I hadn't completely admitted how jealously I was guarding this fantasy, but Dolly saw it immediately, I thought.

"In the subtle world, one sees everything immediately," she said.

"Do you mean that literally?"

"Oh yes. That's why I'm not reading your mind. I know your

thoughts before you have them. And of course I do a little rearranging of what I see."

I backed away a step. It wasn't only Elena who made Circe look like the Easter bunny. "What do you mean by rearranging?" I asked.

"You'll find out when you learn to do it yourself."

Paranoia is the fear that someone knows something you don't want anyone to know. What do you call it when someone knows *everything* you don't want anyone to know? In the buzzing sound-and-light show of our minds, no tape is more popular than "You don't understand me. Nobody understands me. I need to be understood or I'll never be truly happy," which runs pretty constantly in many people's heads. Dolly understood everything about me, and the idea made my tape get twisted in the sprockets. *Everything is too much.*

"Don't repeat what I'm thinking anymore," I said. I could hear that my voice was shaky.

"All right," Dolly said mildly. "You see why people stay out of the subtle world. It's much nicer to dip in for a bit and then leave. Only people like me and Elena have taken out citizenship." Dolly laughed and looked around, as if invisible beings (more citizens with permanent visas?) were there in the hallway.

Whoever might be mingling, I wasn't included. The distance between me and Elena opened into a wide, black gulf.

"Don't worry," Dolly said, interrupting my gloom. "She loves you."

I felt a spurt of happiness, but it was just a road bump. "What do you mean?" I said suspiciously.

"She loves you," Dolly repeated. "She has love for you. Love is the feeling that for you she has."

I held up my hand. "But I don't get a choice. The kind of love you're talking about shines down like an endless, sunny day, and it shines on everybody the same. It's like a perfect climate that people stop noticing after a while." *And Elena will never fall in love with me*, I thought.

"You're right, she's beyond that. I taught her well," Dolly said, not heeding my warning to stop trampling around inside me.

You're a tricky old thing, I thought bitterly, but what I said was, "Can you make me feel better about this?"

Before she could reply, the door opened, and Elena appeared with the portable phone in her hand. She handed it to me.

"Sorry about that, but your apartment is awfully small," she said apologetically.

"The door's thin, too," I said. "I could have been beaming bad karma through it."

She gave me a quizzical look and took Dolly by the arm. They began heading for the elevator. Picking up the bags, I said, "Forget that remark. I got a reminder while I was waiting out here."

"About what?" Elena said.

"About not taking you for granted."

She smiled, but I knew I wasn't at peace. Some part of me now looked on Elena as a kind of sacred monster wrapped in the guise of a young woman. She was a mystery, and mortals do best by shunning mysteries.

"You know I could easily be afraid of you," I said.

Elena raised an eyebrow, but she didn't deny it. I felt my heart give a nervous flip, and I said, "I think this is the moment when you're supposed to say I have nothing to be afraid of."

"You have nothing to be afraid of," she said. "And remember to call your sister about Thanksgiving."

"What should I tell her?"

"That you've found an attractive woman of the right age to

bring along." A wistful note entered Elena's voice. "I haven't eaten the right kind of Thanksgiving dinner in a long time."

I pointed my nose toward the elevator, and got the two of them inside with their luggage. They were gone without waving, and I forgot to ask where they were spending the night. But I felt better. This wasn't good-bye, and despite all the wisdom Dolly had dispensed, I still harbored a goodly store of foolish hope.

THE NEXT DAY didn't begin propitiously. Elena and Dolly remained out of touch. I hung around waiting. I watered some desiccated plants that would have survived if I'd watered them last month but were now a lost cause. I picked up socks from the floor and threw them back again. What faced me was pretty obvious. I had to return to work. There wasn't much alternative except to pretend I had my normal life back.

I visualized the backlog of news copy and feature articles on my desk. When I finally phoned in, Cuddihy, the managing editor, wasn't exactly thrilled to have been left hanging. This was Wednesday, and I had been out of touch since Friday afternoon. I promised that I'd come in and stay as long as it took to catch up. Because I was normally in his good graces, Cuddihy grudgingly accepted. But still I dawdled. Ever since the moment my eye caught the tiny ad in the Sunday paper, I had been riding on a wave of secret excitement. Now it was deflating. The two women had taken it away, who knows how. Even my anxiety over Elena concealed a thrill that I'd never known before and didn't want to lose.

By 10:30 I made it downstairs. On the way out, I dropped off an extra set of keys with Ruben, the super. I didn't want Elena to show up and miss me. I described her, and Ruben gave me a sly smile.

"Congratulations," he said.

"It's not like that."

Ruben spread his hands wide. "Guys like you and me, amigo, we can hope. It has to be 'like' something." Ruben had a wife and some kids back home in Guatemala.

I went into the T, taking the orange line a couple of stops— just a hop, but it felt like traveling to the wrong galaxy. As I stood at the rear of the train looking out the back window, everything magical disappeared into the darkness of the tunnel as if it had never existed.

Staring up at the building on Stuart Street where I worked, I could have sworn that crews had spent the weekend making it look ugly and cold. My stomach knotted up at the thought of reentering the newspaper offices on the fifth floor. In my mind's eye I could see rows of steel desks lit by banks of buzzing fluorescent lights. I heard the cocky banter of bored reporters playing one-upmanship games that nobody ever won.

The drone of my self-pity lasted all the way upstairs. I skipped the elevator, figuring that if I ran up five flights my body would kick start some kind of energy. It didn't. When I reached the landing that led to the newsroom I sat down on the top steps.

Seconds later, one of the young interns, Rebecca with the ponytail, burst through the metal door and almost collided into me.

"I didn't see any copy from you this morning," she said.

"Don't sweat it," I grumbled.

"Hey, I was only saying . . ." Rebecca stepped around me and kept going. Her thick clogs clanked on the metal stairs all the way down. I didn't want to move. My fate would be signed and sealed the moment I got back to work. It didn't take an oracle to see that.

You may wonder why I wasn't showing more faith at this point. I'm not that good at faith. My memories of church go back to childhood and the cold disillusionment children can feel. In my case, the exact roots of unbelief are hard to trace. However, I remember singing hymns, which I liked, and being bored in the hard pews. I also remember feeling special when my parents took me behind the altar one Sunday and watched me don a red robe and white surplice; at twelve I was being allowed to help the priest deliver communion. The event had an aura about it. But later that day came the part I remember most vividly, when the church rector said, "Be good and take this out back, will you?"

He handed me a garbage bag that rattled with plastic cups and empty wine bottles. I went around to the alley and heaved them into the Dumpster. The alley stank, and there was a hairy derelict who slept in the corner under a blanket, seeking the refuge of a church alley because everywhere else they beat him up. Some older kids had told me that he wore sharpened false teeth that he could take out and use to snap at you. I was mortally afraid of him, and when I heard rustling in the dimness beyond the Dumpster, I ran for my life. Of course I was running from a ghost, but no Holy Ghost stepped in to stay my fear. I lost any sense of God protecting me at that moment. Nor did I ever regain it.

So if faith was separating me from Elena, I'd never bridge the gap.

You're wrong. You've been initiated.

This new thought struck without warning, and before I could

question what it meant, an image rose from my memory. I saw myself digging up the statue buried in the snow. The sight of the green glade came back, bursting with life, a haze of buds surrounding every tree. That place couldn't have existed. Not unless it was a glimpse of Dolly's subtle world. Which meant that I had entered it, if only for a moment.

Going back to work would be like shutting that portal—I might never find it again. Nobody's life prepares them for an initiation. Maybe one could occur every day, only we don't know how to welcome it. Anyway, invisible doors are as good as locked. Did I really have anything more than a memory of one?

I heard a slam and footsteps on the stairs. Rebecca was coming back up with whatever she'd been sent to fetch—pizza and Coke, usually. When she rounded the last landing, however, it wasn't the intern but Elena. She stopped and held her hands on her hips, panting.

"How did you find me?" I said. I was at a loss, although the sight of her came as a tremendous relief. Some part of me wanted to cry.

Elena herself was in a good mood. "I knew where you were because I never went away," she said.

"Do you watch me from afar?" I joked mournfully.

"Not too far. You needed time by yourself to work it through. How far did you get?"

I pointed toward the newsroom. "I don't think I can go back in there."

She came up the last half flight of stairs and sat down beside me. "That's how it works. One day you are where you belong, and the next day you can't go back."

"But where do I belong now?"

"Wherever you want."

"I don't think that's good enough." I was saying something

pretty adamant. After all, I had confidence in my writing, and earning a living would always be possible. So the thing that caused anxiety was not survival; it ran deeper than that. I had taken a huge step into Elena's world, but I didn't know the first thing about living there.

"What happened to me was a kind of initiation, wasn't it?" I said.

"That's right. You had a breakthrough. One of the reasons you needed some time alone was so you could sort that out. Nobody can decide except you—that's the great gift of being set free."

At that moment, I didn't feel set free. A few glimpses of a strange place on the edge of nowhere doesn't automatically give you a new life. "Tell me what I should do," I said.

"You are responsible for yourself now," Elena said. "Accept what you know. There is a second world, a subtle world, that you've been privileged to discover. Don't turn your back on that gift, ever."

She had been earnest with me before, but this was the first time I heard Elena sound solemn. Being the young one, you would have expected her to be more carefree than Dolly; it was turning out to be the reverse.

"I didn't do anything to you," she went on, "and neither did Dolly. We simply cooperated with what you wanted. We were the midwives who helped you give birth to yourself."

The image made me squirm. I didn't want to be a new mother or a squalling infant. "If I quit my job, I won't have money. If I spend time with you instead of my old friends, if I start acting like I'm special and throw myself into everything the opposite of what I used to do, what's going to happen? I could just mess up my life and lose everything." I felt a squeezing pressure in my chest, because if Elena was saying I had to be on my own, I wasn't anywhere near ready.

"No one's forcing your hand," she said. "If the subtle world is

all around you, there's nowhere special you have to go and nothing special you have to do. That's not what I meant by accepting
the gift."

I asked her what she *did* mean.

"Freedom comes with a price," Elena said. "Breakthroughs
aren't rare—anyone's psyche can be shaken up without half trying.
We're all pretty insecure and loosely strung together.

"It's what you're willing to make of yourself, after the breakthrough, that determines your future. Now you see *what is*. Your
old self had operated with a lot more illusion than you ever realized. What will life become without illusion?"

"But I don't see *what is*," I insisted.

"It may take time."

"And what do I do today?"

"Whatever you want."

Why did she keep saying things that were supposed to be reassuring but only shook me up? Although a part of my heart was
elated, because I was in Elena's world and she accepted me there, I
still felt alien. "I didn't ask to be initiated," I reminded her.

"Sure you did."

"When? Tell me exactly."

"There's no exact moment," Elena said. "You ask before you're
born. You come into the world to achieve it. And now you have.
You've achieved something great, believe me. People who consider themselves seekers of truth go all their lives without getting
what you have. Now we'll see. Initiation is a beginning, followed
by many, many events to come. The best way I can put it is that
you've made a change of level. On the old level, certain rules held
you back, and now you don't have to obey them anymore."

This was all sounding better, but it didn't answer my apprehension about going back into the newsroom. I kept worrying that
Elena was pointing me to a way of life that sounded beautiful but

unrealistic. Where would it leave me if I gave up everything I knew? After everything I'd been shown, there was still a primitive side of me that was paralyzed. I could even see it as a scared, balky child whom I pictured like this:

Imagine that you know a very unusual two-year-old. You are visiting his parents, and when they leave the room, he says, "I'm worried." What does a two-year-old have to worry about, you ask. "Books," he says. This sounds unlikely, but he looks very anxious. So you ask him why he's worried about books.

"I took a peek at one, and it's covered with black specks on every page," he says. "I'll never understand what those zillions of specks mean."

You tell him that the zillions of specks will make sense one day. The only thing he has to do today is play with his dolls and coloring books. Things will change when the time is right.

"But how?" he asks. "My brain sees only specks, no matter how hard I try. I want them to make sense. What should I do?"

The answer is that he can't do anything. Books are unfathomable when you can't read, yet one day their meaning begins to dawn. Did some gene kick in? Did the child's brain develop some new wiring? But if your brain can't read to begin with, how could it know which wiring is needed? We all possess the same genes as cave men a million years ago, and they certainly didn't kick back with the sports section. Why would we evolve a useless gene that sleeps for a million years just in case writing might be invented? Maybe this is where faith begins and science hits the road.

I'm not pretending to unriddle this riddle. Sitting with Elena on the newsroom stairs, I only knew that I was about to walk out on my old self without any promise that the new one would have a clue what to do.

"I stumbled into this whole situation," I muttered.

Elena smiled. "Everybody stumbles into it."

"Did you?"

"Don't get hung up on my story. I'm not just some girl," she warned abruptly.

"You think I don't know that?"

"We'll see." The next moment her voice softened. "This whole journey is going to be about love. Love is what allows you to re-make yourself."

Elena remained in a good mood, and she spoke so beautifully that I'm going to tell you the rest of what she said that day. If you're mostly interested in how I turned out, you can skip this part. But how will you turn out? There's the cosmic question . . .

"The fate of each person is too mysterious to predict," Elena said. "But the subtle world is the place where the future waits for us. There, you are young before you are old, dying before you were born. There, the unfurled bud is already open and last year's harvest sprouts from this year's seed. I'm going to be teaching you something special if you want to see such a world. It's a kind of at-tention you have to pay—you can call it subtle attention or sec-ond sight." Elena stood up and began to dust off the stair grime from her skirt.

"Wait, how are you going to teach me?" I asked.

"You'll know."

"When?"

"Soon enough." I could tell she was enjoying this. The only thing that kept my frustration level down was that she said, "As-sume that the subtle world wants you to come in. The veil that separates you is thinner than a cobweb, so there's no question of being too far away. You simply haven't paid the right kind of at-tention yet."

"Did second sight show me the statue in the snow?" I asked.

"Yes, and everything else you think is so amazing. Second

sight feels like magic sometimes, but really it's very natural. You'll be seeing with the eyes of the soul. You've been waiting to do that a long, long time."

Suddenly Rebecca appeared on the stairs below. Neither of us had heard the fire door slam downstairs. She carried a bag of take-out Chinese food in her arms. The warm smell of roast duck and soy sauce wafted up.

"Hey," she said.

"We're discussing Mr. Conover's big break," said Elena.

"Cool." Rebecca wove sideways between us to get past. I was on the verge of telling her that I was quitting, but Elena squeezed my arm. The intern disappeared through the door into the newsroom.

"My big break?" I said when she was gone.

Elena laughed. "Well, it is. It's your time. Here, take this," she said, handing me a card. It was from one of the expensive hotels on the other side of the Boston Common. "You can reach me there. I have to get back to Dolly now."

After she left, I opened the door and went into the newsroom. A few people looked up, but no one commented on my absence. I found my desk piled as high as I'd envisioned. I sat down and started rewriting the top story, the one about the homeless camping out in the Fenway. It took me the better part of an hour. When I was through I took the copy and knocked on Cuddihy's office.

"Here," I said, tossing it on his desk. "I'll finish the rest, too, but that will be all. I'm not coming back."

His eyes narrowed. Cuddihy is about fifty, and he's a direct, no-nonsense son of the Irish—whiskey and blood. He said, "You're leaving, boom, just like that? I haven't heard you complaining. If this is about money, let's talk."

"It's not about money," I said. "This whole thing sneaked up on me."

"What whole thing?"

"I've been growing restless."

"Restless isn't a thing." Cuddihy sounded skeptical. "What's really going on?"

Being twenty years older than me and one of the founders of the paper, Cuddihy exercised paternal rights. The paper was his baby, his whole life. He wouldn't blister me if I laid out what had happened over the weekend, because I had been one of the few writers who were there from the beginning. But Cuddihy couldn't possibly get it, either. Rewriting one more story felt completely dead to me; that was the long and short of it.

"It's personal," I said, not much liking my evasion. "Something tells me I have to get out now or I won't get another chance."

"If someone recruited you behind my back, all I can say is that you should have come to me," Cuddihy scowled.

"No one recruited me. I'm not right for this job anymore." I winced, remembering all the times he'd thanked me for my loyalty, for not jumping ship when the paper's finances became rocky, which was often.

There was a long, tense pause, then Cuddihy said, "It's okay, kid. Whatever lets you sleep at night." He looked down and went back to work.

I cleaned out my desk, half in a daze. Maybe you think I was throwing dice with my life. Several voices were screeching in my head telling me just that. But if I was free, as Elena said, I had to test it. I didn't want to pretend to myself. I didn't want to show up tomorrow doing and saying the exact same thing that I always did and said, yet with an inner smugness about being anointed.

The thing is, even as I was taking my courageous step, I knew I'd crumple. Breakthroughs last a little while, and I was in the afterglow of mine. The doubt and negativity would creep back soon.

They'd try and convince me that nothing had changed. What could I show to prove them wrong? I wasn't a paragon of anything. Love, meaning romance, hadn't worked out. My fantasies were hatched in high school and hadn't changed all that much since then.

Let me lower the tone of this narrative a little while I reveal something I'm not very proud of. The first girl I ever had sex with, her name was Janice, was somebody I was fixed up with when I was eighteen. Her habits were known. We smoked some weed and went out behind my parents' house. We sat on a picnic table in the dark talking about nothing, and soon I got lucky. I piled on Janice without even asking the way around. It bore the same resemblance to lovemaking that a three-car crash does to the Grand Prix.

Later when I was more suave, I called sex "flopping the pillows." I forget where I picked that term up. The word *lover* didn't mean "one who loves," not to me or anyone I knew. It meant getting what you wanted, and since girls no longer seemed to demand courtship anymore, both sides seemed to be getting just what they wanted. I thought of myself as one of the nice guys, someone who never made a girl cry or feel cheap. It was a matter of principle with me that no ex-lover went away without remaining friends.

I should have felt a hole in my heart, but that didn't happen—it was more like my heart remained discreetly out of sight. Yet secretly I think it was considering defecting. One time I brought a girl home from a party, and we had sex, but she didn't spend the night. She told me she had to work the next day, which was Saturday. I, being a gentleman, accepted this explanation at face value. She pulled on her skirt and blouse while I watched from the bed. She didn't kiss me before heading for the door, but she had a parting remark.

"We should do this in reverse some time," she said. I asked her what she meant. "You know, instead of let's have sex, tell me about yourself, and then maybe we can go on a date, we could go on a date, ask about each other, and then have sex. That would be a kick." She told me this in a tone of ironic banter, but something hit home: I had never done it in reverse, and I barely knew any guys who understood that reverse used to be forward. Which is my way of saying that other things must have gotten stuck in reverse, too.

Years later, it seemed like a good idea to walk away and find out what forward was really like.

LEAVING THE OFFICE, I headed for the T with my cardboard box of stuff salvaged from my desk, walking through the soft rain toward Boylston Street. You already get by now that the cold is my element. Letting the chilly drops drench me, I laughed recklessly at my good luck. Elena was opening me up. She wasn't in love with me, seemed to have not the slightest interest in the possibility, yet there was no doubt that we were together on this journey. The fact that only three people in the world could make sense of it pleased me enormously.

I didn't start to come down until I was on the subway and became aware that I was soaked and shivering. When I got home and opened the door, my phone was ringing. I ran to pick it up and had to disguise my disappointment when I heard the voice at the other end.

"Did you find your secret admirer?" It was Renee.

"Of course not," I said, not even pausing to consider telling her the truth.

"That's too bad—everybody could use one of those. I wonder what yours would have looked like."

She sounded casual, but Renee is smart and has radar. What was she scoping for? I started thinking fast; I remembered telling her about the ad in the paper—that was the last conversation I could recall.

"You were right," I said. "It was somebody's weirdness."

"So you did go up there?"

"Yeah."

"You sound odd, and you never called again. Are you and I having some kind of trouble?" Renee asked.

"We're fine," I said. "Let's get together. I miss seeing you."

Renee sounded satisfied. "Listen, I know you're having Thanksgiving with your sister, but my mother made a pie, and it's supposed to be a care package for you. Can I run it over?"

"Sure, I'd like that. Your mother always thinks of me."

"I do, too. I'll be there soon."

I hung up feeling guilty. I had worked too hard to get Renee off the phone. Why did I do that? Besides, there was something new in her voice, and I hadn't given myself enough time to figure out what it was. The new note wasn't hostility. It wasn't suspicion, either. Why was I so uneasy then? I gazed out the window at streets left quiet with people going off for the holiday. Dingy patches of old snow lingered in the shadows.

When Renee arrived, I wondered, would she instantly see how different I was? Nobody so far had intruded into the charmed circle Elena had drawn around me. I couldn't shake the feeling that anyone who found out about us would want to trample our secret garden.

After what seemed like an hour, the buzzer sounded from downstairs. I answered, then I took a position near the door so I could open it as soon as Renee knocked. She would think I was eager to see her. Then I thought twice and moved away from the door. If I answered too quickly, it might seem unusual. My worrying proved irrelevant, though, because there wasn't a knock. A key turned in the lock, and Renee let herself in, brushing past me with hardly a look.

"Hey," she said, carrying a paper bag into the kitchen. "Were you standing guard?"

"No, I've been waiting for you," I mumbled.

"Sorry, I was clipping stuff out of the paper. Big sale day coming up."

My nervousness felt ridiculous now that Renee was in the room. In fact I felt an immediate attraction. Her pale hair was growing out for the winter, and without the summer sun it was getting tawny again. The air had a sweet, clean scent as she passed.

She said, "Did you finish that feature on the homeless camping out in the Fens? It's turning really cold, and no one's doing a thing about it. Maybe your story will light a fire under somebody." While she chattered, Renee busied herself unpacking a pumpkin pie wrapped in foil, a plastic tub of cranberry sauce, and another of stuffing. The portions were enough for three.

"Do you want to unwrap this food now, or should I stick it in the fridge?" Renee paused, waiting for an answer.

The moment called for an offhand reply, but suddenly I knew something. *She was feeling hurt.* The knowledge didn't come to me in words or as a deliberate thought. I simply knew, as if feeling her emotion directly in my body. Without thinking, I said, "I'm sorry."

"What do you mean?" Renee looked confused. She turned and opened the refrigerator door to stow the food away.

She's hiding now. I found her out, and she wasn't prepared for it.

This, too, I knew instantly. I mumbled, "I should have called you."

Renee took a moment to stand up from behind the refrigerator door. When she did, her face was blank.

"Call me when?" she said.

"You mentioned over the phone that I hadn't called you back."

"No, I didn't." She stared at me without blinking or changing her fixed expression. I was on the verge of saying, "Yes, you did," but before the words came out, I got another message.

She isn't just hurt about that. There's more, and it's big.

In five seconds, my perception had moved from noticing Renee's scent to uncovering something dark. Maybe much darker than I was prepared for. If she was hurting this much, did she blame it all on me? Or did the wound have nothing to do with me? I couldn't tell. I could only sense an anxious quiver inside her.

Renee went back to arranging space in my fridge for the food she'd brought. "You're not talking much recently," she said. "Have you noticed? I noticed on the phone, which is one reason I came over. I wanted to check on you."

I watched her, not knowing how to reply. Her words were too abrupt, and they carried an edge of accusation—a conscious edge, but if I pointed that out, Renee would deny it, we'd fight, and the fight would be my fault.

"You don't have to check up on me," I said.

She folded the paper bag and looked around for a place to put it. "You always say that. It's one of the things that keeps me checking up on you."

"So if I asked you to check up on me instead, does that mean you wouldn't?"

"No, that's not what it means. You're twisting things." I could tell that she was trying to keep the focus on me. All the hinted-at hurt went scurrying back into the shadows. It was very bizarre trying to follow her on parallel tracks. Despite her best effort, she was getting sadder since she'd come through the door.

"Wait, stop," I said, holding up my hand. "We got off on the wrong foot. Let's go back, okay?"

Renee narrowed her eyes. "You're the one who said we weren't having troubles. What's with you, exactly? Did something happen these past few days? You didn't lose your job, did you?"

"No," I said, startled. Renee kept her radar on; I hadn't been fooling myself about that. "Let's go back to when you came through the door."

Without waiting for a response, I went over and hugged her, hoping to cover up the half lie I'd told about my job. For a few seconds her body was tense, but after a pause she read the embrace as a simple apology and hugged me back. When we parted, she looked more relaxed.

"I can't stay. I was on my way somewhere," she said. "Are you okay by yourself?" Renee's face wore an expression of friendly concern, but it didn't work.

You're scaring me. I have to run away.

This latest message, which came to me as effortlessly as the others, disturbed me the most. I had no awareness of saying anything to frighten her at all. But there was no way in hell I could come out and tell her that.

"Sure, sure, I'm great," I said. "Tell your mom she's my kitchen angel."

Renee gave me a fleeting smile and turned away without a good-bye kiss. The next minute she was gone.

I began to pace. *What just happened?* I felt as if my mind was wrapped in tangled yarn. Renee and I were old friends, old lovers. I had listened to her voice, but I had heard a second, truer voice speaking at the same time. That voice wasn't comfortable with me; it barely knew me. If there were two Renees, which one had once fallen in love with me? Which one had decided to quit sleeping with me and drifted away to be on her own again?

The tangle of impressions refused to unravel. All I could think was that this must be what Elena had prepared me for—second sight. Subtle attention. My mind was becoming like one of those lenses that shows half an image underwater and the other half above the surface. I'd never imagined you could see that way. Much less did I know how to handle it.

IT WAS the first Thanksgiving of my new life. I looked at myself in the mirror while I cleaned up and said the magic words out loud. "My new life."

The phrase gave off a spark, but I wondered how far I could push it. Which part of my life would be new? Which part would refuse to budge? I busied myself in order not to think too much about it. I laid out some good clothes and performed the once-a-year ritual of polishing my black dress shoes. Traditionally this was Linny's day to shine. I had spent more than one Thanksgiving alone before she moved up north. One time I walked through a ground blizzard to get a turkey sandwich from the White Hen convenience store, throwing in a can of cranberry sauce at the last minute. But for the past few years, my sister has had first dibs on me during the holidays.

When I'd finished getting dressed I went back into the bathroom. I looked into the mirror and tried the magic words on again.

"My new life." No one else has to notice, I told myself. No one even has to know.

This was a touch of bravado. Earlier in the morning, I had bought an expensive bottle of red Bordeaux at the neighborhood wine shop, something way beyond the means of a man who had just quit his job. Pushing forty dollars across the counter and getting two dollars change was a jolt. My old life wasn't giving up easily; it kept setting off worried rumbles like depth charges beneath the surface.

Linny wanted everyone to make an appearance at two o'clock, with dinner to begin at four. I went out to get the car. If I picked Elena up a little early, we could stretch the half-hour drive to the shore; the extra time would allow me to get back into inspiration mode.

Elena was already waiting in front of the hotel when I pulled up, a bouquet of flowers in her hands. I leaned over and pushed the door open for her, beating the doorman to it. I wished her a happy Thanksgiving, willing myself to sound put together. Elena, who seemed immune to moods, flashed a smile and got in. The flowers were lilies, and their sweet musk filled the car with Oriental perfume.

Putting the car in gear, I said, "You look nice." The weather had turned mild again, so Elena wore a light outfit, a black dress that gave her pale features the look of porcelain.

"You found a suit hiding somewhere." Elena did that thing of brushing lint from my collar that girls can't resist. "Good choice."

"You should see the guy I had to beat up before he'd give it to me."

This was pleasant, but I expected a secret glance or word, some sign to indicate that we were on a special wavelength. When Elena merely looked contented, I began to fret. I found myself counting the thumps every time the tires hit a seam in the concrete road. After twenty-five thumps, she said, "You're different today."

"Better, I hope."

Elena looked doubtful. "A little more tense, actually. You shouldn't expect to feel good every moment. It doesn't work that way."

I told her about my experience with Renee and asked her if I was tuning in to her through subtle attention.

"I'm sure," Elena said. "You were noticing that part of her that feels unloved. Everyone carries that part around, but they don't show it and we pretend not to notice."

"So I didn't do anything to her?" I asked.

Elena gave a wry smile. "Truth?"

"Of course."

"You bring up her bad memories. You make her unhappy by being what she doesn't want."

"I tried to be what she wanted," I protested.

"I'm sure you did, or at least you took stabs at it," said Elena. "But would that matter? If you always try to be what someone else wants, the one who winds up unhappy is you. Yet if you don't try to be what someone else wants, you will come off as selfish. The relationship falls apart or degenerates into two people sharing space together. It's tricky." Elena said all this quickly, without much show of interest. I was about to call her on the fact that she was not giving me any answers, but she anticipated me.

"Right now this isn't about you and Renee. I'm not here to patch things together for you. And I'm not here to be your answer box, either."

I felt caught out. "What should I expect from you?"

"You can expect me to tell you the truth about the process."

"What is the process?" I asked, feeling suspicious. I've heard that term used too many ways; women in particular seem to "process" their feelings as another name for looking really sad and angry. Then there's the blame factor. As in, "I've been processing what you said, and I now realize that I've been feeling so bad because of what you did to me." But if someone has really processed their feelings, wouldn't the anger and sadness be gone?

Elena sensed my doubt. "Don't get stuck on terms. This is the process of making you real. Use any term you want. Once it starts, I'm here to tell you the truth about what's happening," she repeated. "That's incredibly more valuable than making you feel good. The process doesn't feel good all the time. For a while you're going to keep feeling the way you did before. Mostly cloudy with intermittent sun."

Was she being flip or trying to put things gently? "Why not mostly sunny?" I asked. I noticed that my stomach was beginning to tighten.

"Because you can't look at yourself and feel sunny all the time. It's not realistic. You blame Renee and she blames you back. For what? For making too many problems. Most people go into relationships to feel good, and when that doesn't happen enough of the time, they decide that the relationship must be failing. Right now you're better off not even considering what other people are doing to you. Give yourself completely to the process."

Then, despite the fact that I had been unsuccessful up to now in getting Elena to tell me her own story, she revealed a piece of it. "Everybody starts out excited by the prospect of a new life. They hope the process will feel good all the time. I know I did. Dolly burst that bubble early on."

Dolly—how had I forgotten her? "I haven't seen Dolly in two days. Where is she?" I asked.

"She's fine on her own, don't worry." Elena hurried on with her story. "I was new to the process. Some strange things had been happening to me, and like you I didn't recognize that they were a breakthrough. All I knew was that I almost went crazy. Someone told me that women get their power from how they feel, while men get their power from what they do. I didn't know how I felt, and I couldn't do anything. Some days I felt like an angel sprouting wings, and the next I was quaking inside with fear. I couldn't hold a job anymore and was reduced to doing temp work a week at a time."

"How old were you?" I asked.

"Twenty-three. Fate brought me and Dolly together. She told me I wasn't going crazy, but that a process was starting. It's bewildering to be told such a nebulous thing. Ominous, almost. But clearly I couldn't keep going on the way I was. Dolly said I reminded her of a snake shedding its skin, halfway out of the old one but not yet in the new. I'm afraid of snakes, so she wasn't helping."

"What was she like?" I said.

"She looked just the way she does now. But from the first day, I felt that she had walked every step she was putting me through. That's how Dolly worked. She gave you tests and then watched how you performed, all the time knowing how she had once felt in your place. That brings us to the thing I wanted you to know about. One day I went to her house—the same one she lives in now—and Dolly brought out a pair of shoes. They were bright, flaming red with high spike heels. The moment I saw them I got nervous. 'Don't you like them?' Dolly asked. 'They're very passionate shoes.' 'I like them as long as you don't expect me to wear them,' I said. No, she told me, she only expected me to wear one.

"I went into shock, but Dolly was totally serious. She had me put on one of those street-walker stilettos and totter around the living room. As soon as I could stay on my feet without tipping over, she shooed me out the door. My instructions were to keep one red shoe on everywhere I went for a week."

"Did you go through with it?" I said.

Elena nodded. "I had begun to trust Dolly, and I was a bit in awe of her. Without a clue to what she was trying to accomplish, my pride wouldn't let me go back there and say I'd failed.

"The first day was horrible. I put on a black high heel to go with the red one, but the heights were still too different. Besides looking absurd, I was so unsteady on my feet that I practically fell on my face getting on the bus. People stared, one man whistled, and I imagined constant whispering behind my back. At my temp job, my supervisor took me aside to say that I was dressed inappropriately. I told him that was harassment, and I was left alone after that. Nobody came near me; by the second day, I couldn't even pretend this was a kind of adventure. By the time I went back to Dolly, I felt like a freak. I walked through the door and burst out crying."

"What did she say?"

"She sat there and listened while I told her how humiliated I felt, and then she started laughing. I had expected her to be wise, to tell me some deep spiritual secret. I grew angry and began to complain, saying that I was going to walk out and never see her again. Just as I was at the height of my rant, she leaned over and slapped me on the face. I was stunned. It wasn't a hard slap, not the kind you see in movies when someone gets hysterical. But it caught me totally by surprise. 'Why did you do that?' I asked. 'So you'll notice something,' she said. 'Everything you've been feeling all week—anger, humiliation, shame, self-consciousness, resentment, the whole package—is in you. Nobody caused it.'

"I told her that she was wrong. *She* had caused it, along with all the people who looked at me like I was a freak or crazy. But Dolly told me that if I wanted to truly be free, I would have to realize that outside forces can only trigger our feelings. We are responsible for everything inside us. Feelings are the echoes of past reactions, which live in us until we call for them. It was an amazing moment for me, a turning point."

"You believed her?" I said.

Elena nodded. "Dolly was telling me the truth about the process, as I'm telling you. She called it good news and bad news. The good news is that you get to change everything that's ever gone wrong in your life. The bad news is that you get to face everything that's ever gone wrong in your life."

"Is that my future?" I said, giving a nervous laugh. "Paying for my sins?"

"Not at all," Elena said quickly. "It's like untying knots. Every person is knotted up inside. We're like tangled balls of yarn, except that the threads are invisible. I know you're curious about Dolly and somewhat amused. She may look harmless now, but she was a relentless teacher. She didn't care what kind of mask you wore to make yourself feel comfortable. She introduced me that day to my emotional body. Everyone has an emotional body. It's where we store our feelings from the past; it's like a memory bank that we call on when a reaction is needed. If someone gives you an order and he's too much like a domineering father or if he offended you last week or if his tone of voice reminds you of an old rival in school, you don't have to compute these things to come up with a reaction. The reaction is just there. You retrieve it automatically from your emotional body."

"Why call it a body?" I asked. "Why not just call them my emotions?"

"Investing your emotions with a body is closer to the truth.

Right now you are digesting every experience at the feeling level. You are metabolizing it and storing its energy. Sometimes emotional toxins get stored; sometimes the energy is positive and nourishing. When you need emotional energy, you tap into your emotional body. If you're lucky, you can discharge its wastes instead of holding on to them. The complexity of the emotional body is as great as the physical body's, only we don't see it as important enough."

We were getting close to our exit now, but Elena had one last thing to say about her beginnings. "Dolly used a kind of shock therapy with that red shoe because my emotional body couldn't release what it was holding. Not voluntarily. A huge amount of negative emotion was coiled up inside as tight as a fist, and this was a fast way to loosen it up. Naturally I was bewildered and confused at first, but between my angry outbursts and my tears, she got me to accept the truth.

"Shutting down the emotional body, she said, is the way everyone tries to defend against being hurt. Like a snail drawing back into its shell, each of us has created an armor that we use to wall our feelings off. This armor is invisible, and since we hide behind it in order not to feel anything, our chief attitude is denial. She sent me out with one red shoe because she wanted me to experience something I couldn't hide from, no matter how hard I tried."

"Was she right?" I asked.

Elena laughed. "What do you think? The way I wobbled down the street kept the eyes of strangers on me. There was nowhere to hide, and that's how Dolly wanted it."

"But if you felt that bad, how was she helping you?"

"She forced my emotional body to give up its secrets. I got to experience what it was like to pierce the armor and have everything pour out. It was cathartic; I hated it at the time, every minute. But when I came through, Dolly told me something I'll never forget. 'Your job right now isn't to feel good,' she said, 'it's to be real.'"

"How great is being real if it makes your life miserable?" I asked with a grim smile.

"Being real feels tremendous. It's the only thing worth living for," Elena said emphatically. "But to get there, you have to cut through what isn't real. Dolly and I had an agreement that she would tell me the truth and I would listen. You and I haven't done that yet."

My stomach was still knotted up; I couldn't help but wonder if Elena was going to press some humiliating test upon me. But I managed to say, without much show of nerves, that I wanted her to tell me the truth, too. By this time, we had taken the exit to the shore.

"We're almost there," I said, "and frankly, it's the last place I want to be. I want to talk some more."

Elena smiled. "Don't worry, nobody's ever complained that the process runs out of talk. Who's going to be at this dinner?" I told her it would be Linny, her family, and a bunch of strangers. She said, "Look around and observe. See what your second sight tells you. Try to take in how everyone is acting from the level we've been talking about."

Soon we were turning into the graveled driveway of the big white house on the water's edge. Linny opened the door in her apron. She seemed flustered but embraced me, Elena, and the white lilies, before steering us toward the fray.

"I want to hear all about you," she told Elena, "but I'm part of the fire brigade right now."

We followed her into the garage, where husband Josh was

standing over a large kettle. "Hey," he said. The deep-frying of the turkey was under way, with the bird submerged and the oil bubbling hard, though not volcanically as Linny had feared. But it was alarming enough. Josh looked brave, while various kids were running up to peer inside the kettle, fascinated by the prospect of an impending explosion. A dozen adult spectators milled around with drinks in hand. I knew some from past Thanksgivings; they were a mixture—friends, neighbors, coworkers—of my sister and brother-in-law's circle. I planned to cling to Elena, but Linny was calling her into the kitchen.

I sat down off to the side, wondering what Elena wanted me to notice. Linny's friends, like herself, were contented and basically doing well. Everyone in the room had their secrets, no doubt, and their foibles. Was that what Elena wanted me to uncover?

Much to the disappointment of the kids, the turkey didn't explode. As the bird was hauled out, a cheer went up—the wine was taking effect on Linny's guests. It wasn't doing much for me, though. I kept feeling the same tightness inside that had begun in the car. Just before everyone was called to sit down, I pulled Elena aside.

"Let's make up some excuse. I don't belong here," I pleaded. I cast my eyes around the room. The faces looked relaxed; people had reached that point in the party when social tensions had been smoothed over. A pack of strangers was going to act sociable for a few hours before going off and forgetting each other's existence.

"You're not observing," Elena said. "You're falling back on old reactions."

"Show me what you're seeing, then," I said.

"All right. Hold my hand during dinner, and I'll help you."

"While everyone's looking?"

She laughed. "No one will mind. They'll just assume you can't get enough of your new girl. I'm this year's model."

Apparently she was right. When Linny ushered everybody to the table, Elena and I were put together as a couple. The food was passed around, and no one gave us more than a passing glance. Elena would take my hand, just a few seconds at a time.

I began to see bits and pieces of a group photo. The kids were boisterous and free, barely able to sit long enough to be in the picture, not caring how they looked in it. The adults cared too much. Each one fought, in their own way, to catch the camera's eye, but at the same time they were incredibly anxious, fighting vainly not to reveal what they'd become. In their own way, each one projected an image that passed for the real person. The woman on my left had a shrill laugh, which exposed every bit of resentment and hostility that she thought was hidden behind her frantic sociability. Her husband on the other side was fuming because he felt that his wife was making a fool of herself. He nailed her with his eyes as she screamed about how great the turkey was and what a genius Josh was to hit on this amazing way of cooking it. You could see the husband struggle to hide his belief that he was too good for her.

Did they have any idea that the very thing they wanted to hide was most visible? I had an image in my mind of the two of them eating out in a restaurant. The waiter brings the wrong bottle of wine, and the husband snaps at him. He goes to fetch the right bottle, and the husband makes a remark: The guy is incompetent, he should know how to take a simple order, what are things coming to in an expensive restaurant like this? His voice drips with contempt, and the wife secretly knows that he feels the same contempt for her. But she hasn't got the courage to show that she knows, and the husband is too busy deflecting his abuse to a decoy.

Then there was Linny. As I observed her, I was grateful that she didn't have the same gray, heavy aura as some others at the table. Yet her eagerness to please wasn't really lighthearted. Like last year and the year before that, she bounced out of her chair to refill a plate, pick up a crying child, brush off a compliment with a flirty laugh. But she was slowly wearing out. This year's perform-ance was that tiny bit more tired than last year's. Her role, taken on eagerly in some dim past, was forcing her to show emotions she didn't really feel. Some part of her wanted to rebel; it hated the mask and screamed to throw it off. But the biggest part of my sis-ter, the part that knew it had to conform in order to survive, was winning. In time only a shred of awareness would be left to scream, and she would do everything she could to stamp it out.

"Jess?"

I turned toward the voice, not realizing how deeply absorbed I was. Elena had let go of my hand; with her eyes she directed me to look down the table. Josh had been asking me a question.

"You back with us?" he said.

"Sure, sorry." I asked for the question to be repeated.

"I was only wondering what's next for you. Your friend here says you've quit your job."

Linny, who was foisting a platter of breast meat on somebody's aunt, overheard. "No job?" she wailed, her face losing its fixed smile.

I held up my hand. "Time out. It's okay, I wanted to move on."

"Move on where?" Linny asked. A few of the guests stopped talking. Family tension was in the air. Before I could reply, Elena said, "He's working for me. He's helping me start a school."

"Really? I didn't know Jess was qualified to teach," Linny said. Elena's role in my life hadn't been fully explained to her, and until it was, this year's woman was an object of suspicion. Not that I had any idea what Elena was talking about, either.

"He won't need qualifications," Elena said smoothly. "We're starting something new, a type of school nobody has thought of before."

"You're in Boston. We've thought of every type of school," somebody said.

This got a polite ripple of laughter. After it passed, Elena said, "It's a mystery school. Have you thought of that?"

"Meaning what?" said Linny, who had given up any pretense of not interrogating Elena.

"Since it's a mystery, you'll have to pay to find out," someone cracked. This, too, earned a little ripple. Elena turned to the woman who'd made the remark. "Actually, you're right."

Linny put down her serving platter. "Jess doesn't know what you're talking about. It's obvious; look at him."

"Maybe I see something you don't," said Elena.

"And what is that?" Linny snapped.

I intervened. "Stop fighting over me. It was my decision to quit. Elena had nothing to do with it, but if you ask me what I think, I'm glad. I may not know what a mystery school is, but I'm pretty sure all of you should be going to it."

"Why?" somebody asked. "Because you're better than us?" The kids were wide-eyed, unable to make sense of the sudden passion among the adults. Some guests looked like they were poised to run away.

Elena put her hand on my shoulder to keep me from answering. She stood up. "I'm sorry. I was invited here at the last moment, and I don't know any of you. But I've been watching, and this is what I see. You all lead good lives. You seem to know who you are and what you're here to do. But how true are these answers? How perfect have your choices been?"

Several of the men snorted or smirked; the women sat quietly, looking bewildered. Elena turned to the man across the table, the one who thought he was too good for his wife.

"Have you ever loved a woman from your soul?"

"Come on, it's Thanksgiving, for God's sake," the man said with undisguised annoyance. I would have thought that a few of the others would pile on to shush Elena, but she seemed to hold them despite their uneasiness.

"All right," she said. "But if you reject the question, who would believe that you know the answer? The word *love* makes you uncomfortable, the word *soul* is empty. Someone set out this splendid feast of thanksgiving, but how many of you are motivated by gratitude?"

Anybody else would have been abashed to hear themselves talk this way, but Elena was blazing. A scorched wave went down the table. She looked at each face in turn, and I've never seen a group of people so pinned to the mat.

Suddenly Elena lost the edge in her voice. "None of you is ever going to see me again if you don't want to. You asked me what a mystery school is, and I'd tell you, except that my answer is, it's a place where you learn that love is a mystery. Either that's true, or love is what you're already living, which is no mystery at all."

Elena sat down, and someone said, "I don't get the point of all this." One of the heavier drinkers, who had been studiously pouring more wine, suddenly cried, "Hear, hear." Another man tinkled the edge of his glass with a fork. His wife grabbed his hand to make him stop.

"You should listen," she snapped.

The husband looked surprised. "What's with you?"

"Nothing." The wife was self-conscious about finding herself the center of attention, but you could see something bitter in her. "If I had more guts," she said, "I'd go to this school." Her voice was blurred with wine. "If we had a discussion about how much so-called lovemaking goes on. I mean actual love, not the—"

Her husband cut her off. "Shut up."

My sister Linny was verging on panic mode. "Please, there are children at the table," she pleaded.

Josh spoke up. "Maybe we should clear the room. The air's getting a little thick."

"I agree," the heavy drinker piped up. "These near brushes with the truth make me thirsty." A few people tittered pointlessly.

I waved both hands in the air. "Stay put, we're going." I tugged at Elena's sleeve, and without protest she folded her napkin and got up. Everyone kept their seat as we left. Linny followed our exit with an angry, hurt stare. When I bent over to kiss her cheek, she didn't return the kiss.

You've ruined my show, her eyes said.

INSIDE THE CAR, five minutes passed before I cut the silence. "Did we have a right to do that?"

"Do what?" Elena asked.

"Get at them that way. It was kind of brutal—did you see my sister?"

"Try and clear away your judgments. Something different was going on," Elena said. Instead of rushing to clarify, she waited for me to react.

"I don't know," I said. "Are you suggesting that those people knew what was coming?"

Elena nodded. "Not just knew—they came for the purpose of being confronted. Nobody who lives in a shell doesn't want to break out. Don't pay so much attention to their resistance; it isn't pleasant when the shell cracks."

"But you can't hammer them just because you think they want it."

Elena smiled. "You think it's like a seduction—they say no, but I know that means yes?"

"Wasn't it?"

"No. I had no personal reason to provoke them, even for their own good. You'll just have to accept that I saw what I saw. I'd never lay on a truth that actually hurts somebody."

We drove in silence while I tried to absorb this. After a while I said, "Whatever you did to them, you got me to uncoil. I should be tight as a drum, but to tell you the truth, I feel amazingly good right now."

Elena looked satisfied. "I wanted you to see what emotional secrecy does. When we walked in, I could read your mind. You thought you were in a room of happy, successful people, everyone but you. You needed to open your eyes."

I didn't really know what Elena saw in me, but the process, whatever it was, had to be better than the world Linny wanted me to stay in. It had to be better than sleeping beside someone you once loved but who is gradually turning into a log. Or having to hide the fact that you feel contempt while your wife pretends she doesn't care.

"Anyway, I didn't put anyone in red high heels," Elena said.

"Let's buy some," I said, laughing at the picture she conjured up. But I turned sober pretty quickly. "Is the process always an ego buster?"

"No, that's a fear the ego has, and it will try to get you to buy into it," she said. "For a man in particular, facing deep emotions generates anger to disguise the fear. That puts you at a disadvantage. You've been taught all your life to believe that emotions undermine masculinity, which means you'll instinctively fight the very process that could set you free. A young girl, if she's lucky, isn't taught that her emotions are a weakness. But every boy is taught that. If the lesson isn't taught at home, it's driven in by other boys at school.

"This is a long-standing and very serious problem. Men want power, and as long as power is viewed as a cold, aggressive, impersonal force, they have no choice but to suppress their emotions. When that's the price for power, you'd think that no one would pay it. Too many men are willing to, and there's the tragedy."

"Do women already know that?" I asked.

"Somewhere inside they must," said Elena. "Women aren't spiritually superior to men; I'm not implying that. Women aren't immune from hiding from themselves. But the masculine way, enforcing a denial of feelings, has spread too far. I hope some of those women call me. I think a few of them will, actually."

"So you were serious about starting a school?" I said.

"I didn't walk in the door planning one, but now I can't see any other way." Elena gave me a mischievous look. "Anyway, we promised Linny that you'd be working. She likes you better as a starving writer, but we can deal with that."

"I wasn't starving," I objected quickly. "When do we start?"

"I'll call some people tomorrow." Elena had one last surprise in store, although I should have anticipated it. "You saw how much chance there is that any of those men would ever come."

"Zero to none." I thought for a second. "You mean it's going to be all women? I'll be the only man?"

Now she didn't bother to disguise her triumph. "For now—you'll get used to it. We'll put out flyers, and you can talk to all the eager females who have your phone number. How bad can it be? Let's find out who shows up, and then whatever happens will be right."

It occurred to me, not for the first time, that Elena's self-assurance was astonishing, and yet she seemed to lack any self-importance. I was wrong to think she'd been crafty with me. She trusted that her impulses were right, and she treated me as if I felt the same way.

It was growing dark, and we were back at the hotel. Talking to

Linny would be grim the next time she called. I had no idea how much help I could really be to Dolly and Elena. I had stumbled into a mystery school, and with no other men, I was on my own. As Elena got out of the car, I took a second swipe at bravado that day.

"I don't know how many women are going to show up," I said. "But I'm getting to know what women want."

Elena was huddling in her thin black dress against the evening chill. "In a month, you'll hardly be able to tell yourself apart from a woman. Good-bye."

This peculiar prediction, which she didn't utter like a joke, sent me on my way home.

t w o

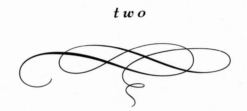

Mystery School

I GOT UP the next morning with a message from Elena telling me to meet her at an address about twenty minutes away. She sounded like she was calling from a pay phone; I could hear construction noise in the background. She gave no other explanation except to come as soon as I got the message. The street was hard to locate. Clutching a map in the car, I wound up in a maze of one-way streets down by the harbor. I spent a lot of time driving past stretches of waste ground and ripped-up railroad tracks.

When I found the right address, it didn't exist. Instead, there was a vacant lot where a building should have been. But Dolly and Elena were standing on the edge of the lot, gazing into the weeds and rubble. They had smiles on their faces as if they loved the view of abandoned tenements, warehouses, and a narrow slit revealing gray, choppy ocean in the distance.

"Should you be here?" I said as I walked up. The wind feels

twice as bitter by the harbor, and both of them were wrapped up in cocoons of wool. "I thought maybe you'd found a building for your school."

"We did," said Elena. "Or rather, Dolly did. She spent the whole day yesterday searching."

"A man in the telephone book knew about this place," Dolly chimed in, waving her arm toward the vacant lot. Her head was swathed in a bright blue boating scarf; the little that showed of her face was beaming.

"You bought this?" I said.

"No, we rented it." Dolly named a price that made me whistle.

"I can see why somebody came out on Thanksgiving to show it to you," I said. "They must be pretty desperate." The lot was jammed in between two crumbling warehouses, and in the distance a construction crew was doing demolition work. They had already been here. A massive pile of bricks about twelve feet high stood where an old building once had been. The lot was enclosed by a high chain-link fence.

"You can't build a school on land you're renting," I pointed out.

"We know that," Elena said. She walked over to a gate in the fence, produced a key, and opened the padlock. Before I could stop her, Dolly slipped through the opening. She carefully skirted the contents of a spilled trash barrel and stopped in front of the mountain of bricks.

"Good, good," she murmured.

I had no business letting her go in. On closer examination, I saw that the rubble heap contained its share of broken bottles and garbage that had been tossed over the fence. You got the feeling that were it not for the construction noise, you would be hearing little scurrying sounds.

"Let's talk outside the fence," I shouted over the din. But Dolly wasn't paying attention. She carefully picked up one of the bricks, walked ten feet to her left, and placed it down on the ground. Elena watched approvingly.

"What's she doing?" I said.

"Moving bricks. Dolly liked this place because it would give everyone something to do."

Dolly walked back to her original spot. She studied the rubble heap as if she was picking out the perfect diamond in a jewelry counter. I couldn't leave her there. I went through the gate and hopped over a load of broken plumbing.

"Can you help me?" said Dolly. She pointed to a brick about seven feet up. "That one."

I clambered onto the pile and brought back the desirable brick, which was identical to all the others. Dolly pointed to the spot where she'd dropped the first one, so I placed its brother next to it. "A bit to the left," she said. I moved the brick six inches to the left. She looked thoughtful. "No, back again." I moved the brick back to its original place. By this time Elena had come over.

"You're shivering," she noticed. I had thrown on the first clothes I could find, and I wouldn't last for long in the bitter wind. Elena pointed at a navy pea jacket thrown over a rusting bed frame. "Wear that for now."

I put the jacket on, but I felt a little mistrustful. "You've thought this out," I said. Over in one corner I spied some diesel barrels with paper and lumber scraps scattered around to start a fire.

"Just like in your story," Elena said.

"I already got that." Dolly was ignoring us, searching the rubble for her next brick. "Give me some idea of what I'm doing here," I said.

"Everything's for the same reason," said Elena.

The process. I suppose part of it is that you're kept in the dark.

I went over to the brick pile and climbed up to fetch Dolly's next choice. I placed it beside the first two, and although she frowned slightly, she didn't ask me to move it.

"Make sure you know which one you want and where it should go," said Elena. "We won't always be around, so you should know that this is careful work. No wheelbarrows, no carrying more than one brick at a time."

"Your turn," said Dolly.

"Right." I picked up a brick from the rubble near my feet. Dolly frowned. "Do you really think that's the right one?"

I was going to reply that any of them was the right one, but that wouldn't be in the spirit of the game. I imitated what she had done, staring at the whole pile to see if a brick jumped out at me. You're going to think the cold was getting to my brain, but suddenly one particular brick sticking out at an angle was saying, *Pick me.* I climbed ten feet to get it and almost broke my neck coming down. Nobody seemed to disagree with my choice, so I put it next to the first three. "Happy?" I said to it.

"It can't hear you," Dolly said. "It's a brick."

Okay. I looked carefully at my chosen brick, and after a moment I moved it a few inches to the right. It felt sort of satisfying in a pointless way—maybe I should rephrase that—in a *pure* way. I went up for another brick and then another. Dolly and Elena made no more suggestions. I attributed this to the fact that I wasn't fooling around. I was anticipating some kind of test, and I thought I could pass this one. I waited until the right brick said, *Pick me,* and when I put it down, no spot was good enough except the right spot.

While I was climbing the pile, Dolly and Elena were huddling. They held a piece of paper between them to keep the wind from blowing it away, and when Dolly unfolded it, they both laughed.

"What is it?" I shouted. I was about eight feet over their heads. Elena waved me off. I continued brick-hunting, but my curiosity was aroused. They had to be laughing at me. I scrambled down and came over to them. Elena had put the piece of paper away.

"Can I see that?" I said. She shook her head. "Why not?"

"It's not finished yet. You'll get to see it, don't worry."

I definitely didn't like the sound of that. "How many bricks do you expect me to do today?" I said.

Dolly and Elena exchanged glances. "Eight," Dolly said.

I was up to six, so I went back and bagged two more. When I put the last one down, I'd made a line. All the bricks in it were equally spaced and the same size. Dolly inspected them, then one by one she picked them up and tossed them back on the pile.

She said, "This one's no good because you were just practicing. This one you weren't serious about. This one you just wanted to get over with. And these two you were thinking about us laughing at you."

"I guess you'll have to start over," Elena remarked.

So I did. I turned around and began staring at the rubble pile again. If you've gotten this far, you probably suppose that picking up bricks is going to be a chapter you can skim. There's nothing to it, and if I manage to find some symbolic value in the act, who really cares but me? I wasn't finding symbolic value.

I selected a brick and brought it down. When I put it on the ground Dolly didn't wait. She immediately picked it up and threw it back. "You were grumbling."

"Right," I muttered, going back again. The next brick got thrown back because she said my mind was wandering, and the next because I was resentful. She waited while I decided what to do.

"We're not stopping until I get eight?" I said. She nodded. "And right now I haven't gotten the first one."

Elena pointed toward the diesel barrels and the lumber scraps. "You can warm yourself after the sun goes down."

Now I was thrown. Would I really be willing to keep doing this until dark? I don't possess a deep well of patience, but at that moment I wasn't about to rebel. I had second-guessed Dolly. I knew about Elena and the red shoe, and how the test was supposed to break you down. In a perverse way, I wanted to see how long it would take before picking up bricks brought out the devil in me. Besides, you can't lose a game you know is pretend.

"You're wasting time," Dolly said as I hesitated.

I looked at the rubble again. I saw a brick that I thought was one she'd thrown back already. I went for it and placed it on the ground. "You did that one," she said. This actually made me feel better; I was right that she was paying attention. I felt a spurt of hope and tried hard to focus on the next one. When I put the brick down Dolly gave it a quick glance and said, "Do you think that's the right one?"

"Why else would I pick it up," I said, "if I didn't think it was the right one?"

"You need to be positive," she said and threw it back.

I did a couple more, and she threw back only one. The one she kept I had picked up with the fantasy of throwing it at her.

"Nice choice," she said. "But I don't think you would have done it."

The construction noise suddenly stopped, and I looked at my watch. Noon break. I considered for a second if finding eight bricks would seriously take me until after dark. My ankles were giving out. The rubble heap constantly shifted under my feet, and keeping my balance was always touchy. My back was beginning to complain, my thighs were twitching in spasms of fatigue.

Out of the corner of my eye, I saw some people passing by.

They stopped to watch as I climbed up the rubble pile. It was two guys in hard hats.

"Did he lose something?" one guy asked.

"You gotta have permission to be in there," the other said. "There's police around here."

"We do have permission," said Elena. I got really uncomfortable coming down the pile with these two guys watching. I put my brick down some yards away from where they were standing.

"I can't see it unless you bring it over," said Dolly. She put a touch of command in her voice. I glared at her, feeling my face growing warm as I picked up the brick and brought it over to her.

"Yes, ma'am," one of the hard hats said.

Dolly threw the brick back. "You hated this one." The two hard hats started laughing as they walked away.

"Don't ever do that again," I fumed.

"Do what?" said Dolly innocently.

"Make a fool of me like that."

She glanced over at Elena, who said, "We can stop now. No one's accomplishing anything." But of course they were. This was the process, right? If I didn't know the right brick and put it down in the right place, I wasn't showing enough trust or faith or intuition. The vibe hadn't hit me; I wasn't in the zone. If I gave up, some other pointless task would be devised to break me down. After a certain point, you become pretty curious about what it will feel like to go completely out of control.

"I'll lock the gate when we leave," Elena said. "So if you stay, no one can bother you." I told her not to—I didn't think being locked in was such a good idea; anyway, where were they going? Dolly was getting tired, she said, so they'd have lunch somewhere and then maybe take a nap.

I waved my hand. "Go, I'll be here." Actually, picking up bricks by myself seemed a lot better to me just then. Elena took Dolly and guided her steps around the trash. From the back, Dolly's head was a bobbing shape in a bright blue scarf. Suddenly it felt queer to have been so angry with a little old lady wrapped up to look like a Smurf. After they left, I realized that I should have offered them the keys to my car, but they had already rounded the corner to find a cab.

I didn't pick up another brick for a while. A few passersby saw me sitting on the rubble but made no comment. The sweat under my jacket was chilling and clammy. I was more bothered by a drifting sensation. I was out of the loop with both Linny and Renee. Neither had left any messages. Not that I knew what I would say to them when we connected. The lead gray sky started to drizzle faintly. It occurred to me that I had been running ahead of myself. I'd been trying to figure out the point of this test instead of just doing it. Dolly must have sensed that. She saw me second-guessing her, turning it into a contest of wills—which of course I could never win, since only Dolly had the power to say that my bricks were a yes or a no.

"You are taking this way too seriously." I looked up to see a woman facing me from outside the chain-link fence.

"What?" I said.

"Whatever it is you're doing. You look grim as hell."

"I'm taking a break," I said, wishing she'd go away.

"Don't let me disturb you." The woman continued to stand there. How could she possibly be interested? She looked to be mid-thirties, fairly short. Her body appeared thick under the brown leather coat she wore; her accent was not Boston but from somewhere in the Midwest. "Why are you picking up bricks?" she said. "I was watching you the first time I came around the block."

"I'm clearing the lot," I said.

"That's a joke, right?"

"Yeah." She was not an attractive woman. Her voice was abrupt and slightly grating. Even at her age, her face was beginning to sag, and I saw wrinkles starting to set in place where she frowned too much.

"I'm Fran," she said. Without asking permission she walked through the gate. I didn't care, really, given the alternative use of my time.

"Watch the nails," I said and told her my name.

Fran picked up a brick and looked at it. "You pick up ones like this or different ones?" she asked.

"Just like that."

She looked bemused and put the brick down. "I like it here," she murmured. "Can I stay and watch you?" She deposited the large canvas bag she was carrying on the ground and tested the rusty bedframe. *Suit yourself,* I thought. My mental state wasn't too inspiring, so I got to my feet and started searching for my next brick. I had considered cheating—making a big heap as fast as I could and daring Dolly to say they were all no good. Except that I was spooked enough to believe that she would do it and make me start all over.

As I climbed the rubble I looked down to see Fran pull a thermos out of her bag. "Coffee?" she said. I shook my head. If I was going to throw myself into the process, I shouldn't be taking coffee breaks. After placing down a couple more bricks, I relented and asked for a cup. It was good coffee. For some reason Fran kept looking at me with a strange expectation in her eyes.

"Do I know you?" I asked.

Without answering, she pointed across the street. On a telephone pole was tacked a white sheet of paper. Immediately I didn't feel good about it. Handing the cup back to her, I walked across the street to take a look. I shuddered at what I saw. Elena had tacked my picture to the pole. I recognized the shot from my passport, only now it was blown up to an eight by ten. My face wore the kind of scowl associated with the ten most wanted. On top of the sheet some words were printed: *The god of love is back.*

Jesus. I ripped the thing down and tried to control myself. Elena and Dolly had been laughing because of this. I was bait for their school—their scheme was more like it. I felt a wave of paranoia. What if they hadn't gone to lunch but were plastering my picture all over town? *The god of love is back.* I saw my friends reading it. No, that wouldn't matter. Any guy who saw it and remembered my face could come up and humiliate me or kick my butt. Dealer's choice. I felt my throat tighten; I was already choking on the shame.

From across the street, Fran was watching me closely. I didn't know how much emotion my face gave away, but she couldn't think I was happy. She continued to gaze. Her own expression was somewhere between blankness and a puzzled frown.

She likes you, said a voice in my head. *Seeing your picture made her feel something. She doesn't know what the feeling is exactly, which is why she came back.*

I could have jumped into my car and gotten out of there; the woman across the street was nothing to me. But despite myself I knew what she was feeling. Yearning. Seeing the poster had caused a welling up of yearning that she couldn't resist. I knew this without thinking, as I had known what Renee had been feeling. Another wave of paranoia washed over me. Hadn't I joked with Elena that I knew what women wanted?

It took a moment before I realized that I was breathing again. Wadding up the poster, I shoved it into the pea jacket and walked back to the vacant lot. Fran, who was starting to look damp in the drizzle, didn't get up from the rusting bed frame.

"Someone played a joke on you, didn't they?" she said.

"No, not exactly."

She looked chagrined and doubtful. "It's okay. I can go," she said and started to pack up her thermos.

"You don't want to leave now," I said. "You'll miss all the action." Without waiting for her reaction, I climbed the rubble pile and found another brick. I took my time, figuring we both needed it. Fran wasn't able to take much more of watching me, however. After a few minutes she got up and handed me a bank deposit slip with something scrawled on the back.

"It's my name and number," she said awkwardly. "You should've put yours on the flyer. It was careless not to, and I'm not fond of careless men."

What could I do? Women were supposed to contact me; that was the agreement I had tacitly made with Elena, and this was her bizarre idea of how to attract them. I tore the deposit slip in half and wrote down my name and number.

"Do we do it at my house or yours?" Fran asked. "I mean, the therapy or whatever you call it." I turned a deep shade of red. Fran picked up her bag. "I suppose I can't trust you to call," she said in parting. "Just don't break into my house. It's not worth stealing from me. There are alarms everywhere, and they mean business."

She gave a tight smile as if she had been making pleasant conversation. Soon she disappeared around the corner. I walked slowly back to my car, reading her full name: Fran Fitch. The syllables felt as stiff as burlap now that I'd met their owner. I opened the door to drive somewhere that served alcohol.

I jumped when Elena, who was waiting in the front seat, said, "That went well, don't you think?"

"Don't make fun of me right now," I warned. "How long have you been here, anyway?" I started the car. Elena let me drive in a grim mood back in the direction of Beacon Hill before saying, "What did you notice about her?"

"Nothing good," I growled.

"I expected more." Elena's tone of genuine regret startled me.

"From me?" I said. "I did everything you wanted. I cooperated with all this crap and got just as burned as I thought I would, but I still did it anyway."

"Think back," Elena said quietly.

I need you. I'm hurting. The words formed as clearly in my mind as before. Fran was a complete stranger, but I knew her instantly. "What did you get me into?" I said.

"You're going to offer shelter to a battered soul," Elena said. "Now you know what compassion feels like. You're beginning to feel other people from the inside. I know it's strange."

"Why did it happen to me now?"

"You're starting to navigate the subtle world. You're paying attention. That's all, nothing magical. Subtle attention comes naturally. Some people tune in all their lives, some never do."

"How much will want to come in?" I asked. I had been deliberately keeping my mind away from Fran. She was trying to tell me how lost she was, how much she needed to turn to me.

"As much as you allow," said Elena. "Some accept the gift and then can't live with it. Feeling your own emotions is hard enough." She gave a faint sigh. "I don't know the whole story with you."

"Why do you need to know the whole story as long as you stay a step ahead of me?" I said.

She ignored the intended irony. "Right now I'm tuned in to your soul more clearly than you are. It won't always be that way. Whatever it tells me to do, I do. You have a choice, though—do you want to go through with this?"

I assumed she meant Fran. "Is the alternative picking up bricks?"

Elena smiled. "It could be. That was improvised until some-body came along. Dolly has her whims."

"Then it was meaningless?" I said, not too happy with her answer.

"You know better than that."

I shook my head. "You can't leave it both ways. What was Dolly's whim about? One brick is just like every other."

"Is one minute just like every other?" Elena said. "Maybe they seem that way, but it's the choices you make that divide one mo-ment from the others or makes a chain of moments into something important or kills a moment so that it ceases to exist. There's a dif-ference between missing the moment, catching the moment, and making every moment count. If every moment was the same, these differences wouldn't exist. But they do, and Dolly was trying to show you why."

"If I look long enough, will the bricks change?" I asked.

"No."

Mentally I threw up my hands. "Then it's basically impossible. You're asking me to see something completely invisible and know for certain that I'm right. So right that you or Dolly or some other supposedly wise person would immediately agree that I've hit on the right choice."

"Yes." Elena always sounded self-assured, and I can convey that, but what is impossible to translate is the calm, simple cer-tainty that she exuded. So try and trust that she never conde-scended to me or watched my confusion with benign detachment. She was like love itself when it's out of reach, a jewel shrouded in mist.

So it was typical of her that having brought me this close to the mystery, she changed the subject. "I think you should call Fran tomorrow, as early as possible."

I felt disgruntled. "I don't know what she's looking for," I said. "Maybe she doesn't, either."

"The god of love, don't you think?"

"Stop it. She's lonely and possibly desperate. Nobody sane would have chased after that poster."

Elena could see that I was embarrassed, and probably she knew how close I came to running away when I ripped down the poster. "You'll be doing this for yourself," she said. "Fran isn't some random woman on the street. She isn't going to be simple. No one ever is, no matter what we tell ourselves—until we get to the end of the process, that is. Then everything's simple. You find out the one thing worth discovering, and once you see for yourself, you wonder how you ever missed it."

"Can you tell me now, before I see it?" I said.

Elena spoke softly. "One might call it a kind of radiance. Behind everything, you suddenly see a luminous glow filling the world."

"You mean it's actually visible?" I said. Elena nodded. "Will you eventually make me see it?"

She evaded the question. "I can open a window for you," she said, continuing to talk softly, as if tapering into a dream. "I saw it very early when I was still too young to tell anyone. I was seven years old, walking home one day. We lived half a mile from where I went to school, but it was a small town and totally safe for me to come home by myself or with my sister, who was a little older.

"That afternoon we got surprised by a rain shower, and my sister deserted me. The downpour filled the gutters with warm, brown water. She ran off squealing, stomping huge splashes as she went. But I hung behind, and as quickly as it came, the hard rain stopped. Over the rooftops I saw a rainbow, with sunlight making the wet brick walls of the houses glow. Over my head it was still sprinkling, however. That must have done it, feeling mist on my face and watching a rainbow at the same time.

"All at once the normal world wasn't there anymore. It was reduced to a flat surface, like a billboard that stretched to the horizon. I was in front of the billboard, and I could see that every tree and house and car was just an image lit up from behind. I had been tricked into believing in three dimensions, and now the trick had stopped working. This wasn't my imagination. The world, you see, isn't *like* a movie. *It is a movie.* What keeps it going is the radiance that projects from behind. If you want to, you can stop watching the movie and look at the radiance directly. No experience is more humbling, and no experience is more real."

"So you were looking directly then?" I asked.

"Not quite," she said. "I was glimpsing. Much later on I got to see the whole thing." If this later experience filled her with memories, she wasn't willing to share those yet.

"How close am I to getting a glimpse?" I asked.

"Ah, don't let me spoil the surprise," Elena replied, suddenly coming back to herself. She rolled down the window and stuck out her arm, letting the cold wind have its bracing effect.

"Spoil it all you want, I don't mind."

She shook her head. "I'll just say that compassion is part of the radiance. Any impulse of love shining through the mask of this world is part of it. You don't have to see sparkles before your eyes, although that's also quite nice. Don't ask me any more questions. What will come, will come. Just remember that you're lucky."

The moment had passed, and she was as pale and composed as before. I kept driving, heading back to her hotel. A thought came to mind that had struck me earlier, only now I knew how true it really was.

Every day is bringing a different world.

It's hard to arrange this book so that each piece of the mosaic fits into the right place. A long time after the events of this day, I ran across something that would have helped me. It was a story of a man who had to pass a test a lot more mystifying and grueling than picking up bricks. So if you're the kind of reader who's tempted to skip to the end of the book before the mystery is solved, here's a big clue to get you to stick with me.

An American who was traveling in the Far East came to Japan, and he somehow got the idea in his head of becoming a Zen monk. His imagination had been caught by reading some books. So he went to a famous old temple and presented himself to the head monk. The American said that he was walking the spiritual path, but his progress was too slow. He wanted to subject himself to real discipline. Did they offer real discipline at the temple? The head monk was extremely polite but told the American to go away. He wasn't cut out for Zen.

The American was young and restless, and since he was already in Japan, he argued hard. Finally, still somewhat baffled, the head monk gave in. He clapped his hands, and someone brought in a black kimono for the American to wear. He was told to go off and see the head gardener. The American hid his disappointment, because he didn't see how gardening would be any kind of discipline. Soon he found out. The head gardener told him to take a bucket and climb under the latrines. After filling his bucket, he was to take the contents and spread them over the flower beds. "How long do I do this?" the American asked. The head gardener didn't answer.

It was a hot August day, and the stench under the latrine was unbearable. The young American didn't even want to start, except that he saw another Zen monk, who looked to be about five years younger than himself, already hard at work. Despite the disgusting nature of the job, this monk looked calm and peaceful. He didn't talk or complain; he didn't shirk his duty, just filled one bucket after another.

I want to be peaceful like him, the American thought. So he climbed in and began to work. The task was much worse than he ever imagined, but he stuck to it, and by the end of the day he was sick to his stomach and totally fed up. The young monk bowed to him and left. The American considered bolting. All he had to do was jump the fence and he would be on one of the main roads leading to town. Then he remembered the serenity of the young monk, so he cleaned himself up and went in to dinner.

Dinner, unfortunately, was torment. The monks sat in two rows facing each other. They sat cross-legged, which the American wasn't used to, and his calves hurt so terribly that it was a blessing when both legs went to sleep after five minutes. No monk was allowed to touch his food until the head monk gave the signal. Despite his ravenous hunger, the American was forced to sit still for a long time before the signal came. Even then he couldn't eat except in a proscribed way. Before him was a bowl of rice and a bowl of green tea. First he had to take one bite of rice with his chopsticks, moving them in the same precise pattern as every other monk was using. Then he had to take one sip of green tea, again lifting it and bringing it to his lips in two precise motions, exactly as every other monk was doing.

The American toughened himself and followed this rigid routine. He was famished, and by the time he'd finished his rice and green tea, he felt hungrier than when he'd started. But at least he could pride himself on accepting the discipline, which after all was what he was looking for. He slept on hard mats that night, only to be woken up at three in the morning. Silently the monks assembled again in the dining hall with a bowl of green tea in front of them, but no rice. The American was groggy with sleep. As much as he wanted to, he couldn't hold himself erect, and his legs hurt much worse sitting cross-legged than they had at dinner. There was a kind of posture policeman coming toward him, a monk carrying a long stick. He whacked the American hard on the shoulders, making him sit up straight. The blow hurt, and after getting two more whacks before drinking his green tea—again in the slow, precise ritual that brought one sip to his lips at a time—the American found himself emptying a latrine at four in the morning in pitch darkness.

He was in a place worse than hell. The first week almost broke him. His body was one massive throbbing ache. His mind rebelled at the stupidity of his task, which was always the same. He began to hate the serene young monk who never spoke. Worst of all, just over the wall he heard people laughing and talking as they passed by; he saw the roofs of holiday buses and smelled cooked food wafting on the breeze. Yet by the second week, the American had found a core of iron, and he stayed.

A month went by. He became used to the painstaking rituals. The posture cop no longer hit him quite so often with his stick. The life of a Zen monk became almost bearable. Except that there was no inner peace, not even a shred. The American had stopped being angry all the time, and he mostly succeeded in fending off self-pity. What was defeating him now was boredom. As he filled his bucket and spread muck over the flower beds, there was ample time to think. He thought about home and the people he'd left behind; then he ran through all the vivid memories he could bring to mind. There were certain fantasies that could be used to while away an hour. Yet after two weeks, the American was shocked to find that he had exhausted the contents of his brain. Everything worth thinking about had run through his mind three if not four times. There were no new sensations around him, just a bunch of monks in black kimonos who didn't pay any attention to him.

By the end of the first month, his boredom had become crushing. The American was appalled at how difficult it was to live with no company but himself. He began to think that his impulse to come there was a mistake. Yet he knew that if he gave in to weakness, there would be no second chance; he'd never voluntarily come back to this place worse than hell. So for another month, he persisted, only to find that boredom changed to depression. His body felt dull and heavy. He took weary, listless steps as he carried his bucket the short distance from the latrine to the azalea beds. If he could have summoned up the energy, he would have been frightened about his health. *A diet of rice and green tea can't be good for you,* despite the evidence that the other monks looked strong and active. *To hell with the other monks*—the American felt disgust with them and the whole enterprise. Sheer fatigue kept him from screaming, and although his mind rattled like an empty can, the absence of thinking hadn't helped. He felt a kind of silent agony that made boredom look like a blessing by comparison.

Who knows how much time passed? One day was the same as another. He was just a ragged black crow merged into a flock of ragged black crows. The only special day was the one when he woke up and realized he would flee. Straggling into the dining hall at three in the morning, the American knew with utter certainty that the next bite of rice and the next sip of green tea would kill him. It was over, and once he knew it was over, hope sprang up in his heart. In two days, he would be on a plane back to a sane country like the one he'd been born in.

He sent word that he wanted to speak to the head monk. Audience was granted. The American took his cross-legged position, which was easy for him now, and told the head monk that he was going. The head monk listened in silence. Seeing his blank face, the American realized that this man didn't care one whit if the stranger came or went. None of the torment he'd been through mattered, and the moment he was gone he would be forgotten.

This realization filled the American with rage. He rose to his feet and began shouting at the head monk. Obscene rage that had been bottled up for weeks poured out—he had no idea what he even said, only that his contempt and fury knew no bounds. The head monk listened impassively. He didn't get up to bow or even nod his head when the American stormed out.

Running through the gardens back to his room, the American was still in such a fury that he wanted to burn the whole place to the ground. He rounded the corner past one of the largest azaleas on the grounds, one that he had spread manure under many a time. It was just coming into blossom, and the American's gaze was distracted. The azalea flower was bright pink, but as he stared at it, the color began to glow with an inner fire. The glow spread to the whole bush, then to everything around him. All at once the American couldn't breathe. It was as if the entire world had caught on fire. Some invisible dam had burst, and life gushed through the gap, creating such a blaze of intense bliss that he could hardly bear it.

The American turned around and ran back to the hut of the head monk, who was sitting in the same position as when he left. "What's happening? What is this?" the American exclaimed. He was so overwhelmed that he thought his head was about to explode. The head monk gave a barely perceptible shrug.

"It takes all this nonsense," said the head monk, "just to open our eyes."

I DIDN'T GO HOME that night with much enthusiasm about Fran, and by the next morning what little there was had leaked away. I could have gotten lucky. The odds, I told myself, were definitely against her calling me. Who was I? A man whose face she'd spotted on a poster. She would have come to her senses and have nothing more to do with me. But she didn't. A message, brief and nervous, was waiting on my machine when I woke up. She had left it at 2:30 A.M., apparently after struggling with the decision in the midnight hours. I listened, standing there in my pajamas.

"Hi, I'm the woman from this afternoon. Yesterday afternoon. I'd like to see you. Maybe someone put you up to this, I don't know. Anyway, don't call if you don't want to. Okay, bye."

Her hesitancy gave me a way out, but I thought about what Elena had said about compassion, and even though a part of me warned that compassion could lead to disaster, I phoned back. When she heard my voice, Fran got even more nervous than in her message. She agreed to see me around three at her apartment, which was less than a mile away, in the heart of the South End. After I hung up, I couldn't fool myself. Fran's problems were lurking barely under the surface. I didn't know any details yet, but I got the vibration clearly enough.

The sinking feeling persisted as I walked up the stone steps to a narrow three-story row house off Tremont Street and rang the bell. I was buzzed in. When I got to the third floor, the door was open. Fran stood just inside. She wore the same quizzical frown I had noticed before, but she was wearing tailored clothes—a suede skirt and a light-colored silk blouse—which was alarming. It confirmed to me that she considered this a date. I reminded myself to use the word *platonic* as soon as I could fit it into the conversation.

"Come in, just don't expect a lot," Fran said. She turned and walked down the short entry hall of her apartment, disappearing around a corner. I found her seated on a gray couch in the living room. She pointed to a plate of cheese and crackers on the coffee table. "We're both probably wondering why we're doing this," she said nervously. "But at least you don't have to starve." I sat opposite her on an identical gray couch and declined the food.

Fran frowned more deeply and started to pour some wine. I looked around at the room, which was well furnished in gray and beige—either Fran hated risk or had decided to decorate around her depressed mood. Objects were neatly arranged on shelves, and there was no evidence of dust. It was hard not to write a caption under this picture: "Extremely Neat Single Woman Waits to Be Rescued."

"Whatever you're expecting, I'm not scary," I said, taking the wineglass Fran held out. "I'm not on a mission, either." If I thought this would put her at ease, I was badly mistaken. Fran went tense. "I just meant that it's okay to take things as they come, get to know each other," I said.

Fran nodded without relaxing at all, and I searched for something to say next. She beat me to it. "Do you go around putting up your picture like that?" she said.

I tried not to wince. "That was the first time."

"It caught my attention, calling yourself a love guru or whatever you said. My other therapists didn't advertise. None of them put up signs." Talking was calming her nerves a bit. She took a long sip of wine. "I don't think they ever went outside, to tell you the truth."

"I'm not a therapist."

Fran looked baffled. Inside I wondered why I didn't let her keep on thinking what she wanted, since the real story was too outlandish to explain. "I don't know anything about neurosis," I added. Another bad step. Fran looked away and smoothed her skirt. The word *neurosis* wasn't one she wanted to hear. Her small restless hands were like birds that couldn't find a place to alight. She said, "I tell you what—"

I interrupted. "I put up my picture because I wanted to help someone. It was a shot in the dark. I've never done anything like that before, but my intentions were good. Please believe me."

As reassurances go, this one was rushed, but the feeling behind it was sincere. I couldn't quite tell where the words came from. If it was compassion, I hoped compassion wasn't about to dig me in deeper. Then I heard myself say something I wasn't remotely prepared for.

"I think love can do a lot more than people think. Love should change everything. I didn't call myself a love guru; I said love is a god because we should be devoted to it. If love is anything less, who cares? I mean, seriously, who cares?"

Fran was wide-eyed now, staring at me with her wineglass poised halfway to her lips. "Wow, mister," she said.

A thought flashed through my mind. *Elena.* She was making me say these things. But more words were ready to come out.

"There has to be a way to make love count. Love feels good, but I can feel good a lot of other ways without being humiliated and rejected. Maybe you've experienced the same thing. Anyway, if love isn't a god, it's nothing."

I jumped to my feet, knocking over my wineglass. Fran's gaze automatically went to the carpet as a dark purple stain spread across it. "I'm sorry," I mumbled as she got on her knees and began to dab at the spot with a paper napkin. She looked up, but instead of scorching me or shouting that I must be crazy, she was smiling.

"You can't go now," she said softly. It was a meek request; her voice had lost all its edges and corners. I slumped back onto the couch. I was too bewildered to pay attention to her reactions. She gave up on the carpet and faced me over the coffee table.

"I'm divorced, but I'm not on the make," she said. "We can both relax."

"That's good," I repeated mechanically. I took a refill of my glass and was grateful when Fran began to do the talking.

"My ex-husband works downtown in one of those big bank buildings. His name is Mitchell," she said. "He liked to take care of me, and he was a good provider. Every year he made more money. He bought me a nicer house than I'd ever walked into. I didn't look the way I do now. Back when we met, Mitchell ran after me like I was the prize of the universe. But he was a bastard"—her voice momentarily regained its hardness, and Fran paused a second while it went away—"I still think about us a lot. All the time, in fact."

She got up and walked to the kitchen, returning with a roll of paper towels and a bottle of spray cleaner. She knelt down again and talked as she scrubbed at the purple stain. "We had six years together, first in Chicago, then here. A year ago, Mitchell left me for someone else."

She paused and said, "Won't you ask me something?"

I faltered. "I don't really know what to ask you."

"Ask if Mitchell mistreated me."

"Did he?"

"No more than any other husband who cheats." Fran quit scrubbing. "It's not coming out," she said. I told her she should call somebody in and send me the bill. "No, that's okay," she said. "I'll pretend it's Mitchell's blood." Fran began to chuckle, at first grimly, but then something caught hold. "I'm sorry," she said, "I don't really want his blood on the floor. I'd have to buy another bottle of cleaner." The chuckle that had been tight in her throat turned into a real laugh. Trying to stand up, she lost her balance, landing on her butt with her legs spread out.

"Oops," she said. Despite herself she laughed again, harder this time. The fight to hold it in twisted her face.

"Are you okay?" I asked.

"It's just a mishap, or maybe it's a mis-oops," she said. "That's it. I'm Miss Oops, I am." Fran began laughing from her toes now, and her body doubled over. The word *oops* got caught in her brain, and she kept repeating it over and over. "Oops, oops, oops" became one long nonsensical word.

"You're sure you're all right?" I said, but it only set her off again. Her bosom shook and tears rolled down her cheeks.

"Oh my God, why is this so damn funny?" she gasped. I couldn't tell what might have been sobs from convulsions of laughter. Eventually it all died down. When the eruption had run its course, she could hardly breathe.

"Oh boy," she whispered weakly. "Who knows where that came from?"

I gave her a hand up. "That was pretty good," I said.

"Wasn't it?" Fran smoothed her hair, which was stringy and

damp with sweat. "Wasn't it, just?" She wobbled backward a step and plopped onto the couch. "Let me pull myself together here. You didn't know you were coming to the fun house, did you?"

The tension in the room was gone. I felt a new energy in myself, an urgency to connect with this woman who was willing to quake with sorrow and laughter. "Let's go on, don't stop," I said. "Mitchell. Did he cheat on you more than once?"

Fran heaved a sigh, coming back to herself. "Almost the whole time we were married. An ex-girlfriend who never disappeared. You know the drill." The last sentence was mumbled into her glass as Fran took a long sip of wine. The reminder brought bitterness back into her voice. "He was better at being a bastard than I ever gave him credit for. Color me stupid."

She was drifting off, and I didn't want to lose her. "Just because your husband cheated doesn't make you stupid. I'm sure you loved him."

Fran opened her mouth wide, and another gale of laughter emerged. Only this time it was ferocious. She laughed as loud as a donkey brays. The ugliness of it pinned me to my seat, but Fran seemed helpless to resist the impulse. Her eyes apologized even as her body gave in. The second outburst subsided, and she flung her head backward. "This is unbelievable. What are you doing to me?" she said.

"It's not me." I was getting alarmed. Fran looked completely wrung out now. She waved her hand, which was limp as a flipper. "I didn't mean it that way. This is great," she said. "Keep doing whatever you're doing."

Her voice faded, and she closed her eyes a long time. I began to think she might be asleep. Checking out would be good for her.

Then I began to realize something. A faint presence had entered the room, like when someone famous or powerful enters a party. The air was charged, and it made your senses ultra-alert. I wasn't doing anything to Fran, but neither was Elena. There was no spell at work, only this invisible force. Things were being drawn out of us that we never intended, though I didn't have time to figure this out then. After a moment, Fran slowly sat up and dabbed the sticky trail where tears had rolled down her cheeks. She said, "Why did you bring up the fact that I loved him? I used to call myself a romantic, but I think you're a worse one than me."

I didn't reply, but she didn't need me to. "I've been working like mad to get over love, and now—" Fran cut herself off. "Oh God, so much is coming back." Her lip began to quiver, and it took a second for her to regain control.

"I don't need anyone to talk to me about love. When Mitchell left, he was giving me a gift. I'm not kidding. Being alone is a gift, isn't it, when the other person has been deceiving you?"

She looked wrung out. I was sure the faint presence in the room was humming. You know how a tuning fork can make glasses vibrate from a distance? It's called sympathetic vibration. That's what was going on. The presence in the room was creating a sympathetic vibration in Fran. When she spoke again, her body no longer struggled against what wanted to come up. After all the convulsions, she sounded almost eerily clear.

"If my husband ever loved me, why did he lie about his money and squirrel half of it away in a Swiss bank account? Why did he talk me into signing over my half of the house, saying that it was for my own protection? I know why. He never kept a mistress out of passion. He was calculating and selfish from the start. Mitchell had to defend himself against the day when I found out what he was up to. He knew that I would be useless someday, but he underestimated me. I got even. My lawyer wound up being fairly impressed. You probably underestimate me, too."

Fran finished her story with steely precision. She wasn't having trouble controlling her emotions anymore. Now there was a numbed detachment, as if she had been recounting facts about someone who had since moved far away and left behind an empty house.

I listened with the hope that the right words would come out of my mouth again. Fran had spun through too many feelings and was hiding too many more. I didn't know how to handle her. "I'm sorry I can't help you," I mumbled.

"Don't be." Her voice and face were completely vacant. Whatever might have happened next, didn't. Instead, the phone rang. Fran glanced at the caller ID. "I have to get this," she said. She picked up the phone with her back to me. She spoke in monosyllables at first, but after a moment Fran's end of the conversation heated up. "I told you this would happen. You always give him money. You don't remember what I told you the last time? That's right, but you didn't, did you?"

This instantaneous return to bitterness and resentment threw me off. *What does she think she's doing?* I thought. Fran wanted to be loved. She wanted someone to care deeply about her and tell her so. However, Fran did everything she could to repel loving attention. She didn't seek the right people to ask love from, and if they happened to come her way, she didn't reveal to them how much she was in need.

Fran was finishing her conversation now. "That's better," she said. "That's what I want to hear. Now I have to go." When she faced me again, her expression was defiant. "Yes, someone relies on me for advice. You can laugh now."

"It sounds like they rely on you a lot," I said, not taking the bait.

"My best girlfriend has trouble with men. More than me, if you're thinking that's possible."

The presence that had been in the room was ebbing away,

pushed out by Fran's return to her harsher self. I felt baffled and powerless, until something struck me. It came so suddenly that I had to force myself not to spill the whole thing.

I asked Fran to get a piece of paper and a pencil. She looked puzzled but got what I wanted, and I drew a large circle filling the paper. "Think of this as a pie. Divide it into pieces, one for each person who's in your life right now," I said. "Name each one as you go."

I could read a host of objections in her face, but Fran divided the circle into six wedges, each labeled with a name. She paused and added two more.

"My parents," she said. Her face had gone back to being a neutral mask, the way it was when I walked in. "Is this some kind of game?"

I told her she could look at it that way. "Before, when you were talking about Mitchell, I felt something in the air. Did you?" Fran looked doubtful. I continued, "I think it was the same kind of energy people feel when they're in love. It was breaking through all the old stuff you were carrying around."

She could have said, "This is too weird," but Fran kept looking at me, and a glimmer of trust showed through the mask. "You felt it?" she asked.

"Absolutely. I told you I wanted to help someone, and this is how. By inviting in something bigger than either you or me. It came by itself when you were convulsed with laughter, and now it's gone. But maybe we can ask it to come back."

"You want me to have some kind of fit?"

"No, I think that happened because you were caught by surprise. I think something gentle and wonderful will happen now."

I had never said such things before, but I had a sense that I was unerringly right. A flash of insight had entered me.

You don't have to look for love anymore. It's already looking for you.

I felt the thrill of this idea the moment it struck me, because it applied to anyone, including Fran. Yet I couldn't communicate it directly. The insight would make no sense to her. I knew she was apprehensive about me at that moment, so I was going around her suspicion and nervousness.

"What do you want me to do?" she asked hesitantly.

I picked up the paper. "I'm going to read each name you wrote down, and I want you to rate how much that person cares about you."

"Why?" Fran looked alarmed.

"It will be like a map. When we're finished, we'll know who you trust, who you get affection from, who loves you and respects you. These are the ones who bring you that same energy that was here. Once we find the right person, you will know where to turn for what you want."

"How do you know what I want?" she said suspiciously.

"I don't. But I think you might not, either. You're still caught up with the feelings from your divorce."

"What did you expect?" said Fran, growing more hostile.

"Nothing. Everybody draws in when they're hurt, but when you squeeze up too tight, love can't find you. There are people who want to send you a different energy, though. They are reaching out, trying to pierce through your sadness and pain. We need to know who these people are in your life."

When Fran said nothing in reply, I figured that the moment had to be seized, all the more since I had no idea where my words were coming from or when they might dry up. "You ready?" I said quickly. I glanced at the name she had written down first. "Joseph." Fran didn't stir, and I held my breath.

"That's my stepbrother. You want me to rate him from one to ten?" she said slowly. "I can't. I don't know how much he'd say he cares about me."

"Don't worry about his answer. Just tell me how much comes through to you."

After a moment Fran said, "Six."

"Margaret."

A long pause. "That's my mother. I thought you weren't a therapist. Eight. No, seven."

"Lizzie."

"Five."

"Madison."

Fran became somber. "Three. She would kill me if she heard me say that. She would think it should be a lot higher."

"Jeffrey."

Another somber pause. "I want to change my mother to a four," Fran said. I changed the number and repeated the next name, but this time Fran gave no answer at all. Her face trembled. "This is a stupid game," she said in a hoarse whisper. "Nobody cares enough. I was faking those numbers."

"I'm sure someone must care," I said gently.

She flared up. "You don't know anything!" I expected her to start crying, but instead she made an effort and calmed herself. She had something to tell me. "I used to imagine that I was stranded on a desert island. No one could get on or off but me. I collected pictures of exotic islands, and whenever I saw something breathtaking, I'd add it to my island. Every feature was real—blue waterfalls, black sand beaches, mangos falling from the trees."

"Your own private Eden," I said.

"More like my air supply. Somehow there was never enough oxygen where I was." Fran looked away and for the first time her eyes, which had been fixed on me like surveillance cameras, turned inward. A dreaminess had entered her voice; she barely seemed to be aware that I was in the room.

"I could breathe on my island, and only one person at a time was allowed to come with me. You know who I picked?" I shook my head. "Never my parents," said Fran. "My parents didn't know how to treat me. They didn't know how to treat each other. Don't ask me why they're like that; I'm not educated enough to tell you. We were stuck with each other in a house of screaming and long, angry silences. We froze each other out or burned each other to a crisp. Fun stuff like that."

Fran stopped and waited for the pain of her recollections to ease. "A kid can't figure out why Daddy storms out for hours at a time or why there's the sound of crying from behind a locked bedroom door. All I knew was that whoever came with me to my island had to really love me."

"Were they imaginary?" I asked.

"Oh no, I took my girlfriend or a new boy I had a crush on. I took my aunt who later died. I even took Mitchell once. I met him when we were barely in college." Fran was able to say her ex-husband's name without vehemence this time. "Now you hand me this game"—she pointed at the paper—"and there's nobody left. No one deserves to go to my island anymore. Isn't that sad?" She said the last sentence in a tone of sour irony.

"Maybe they care for you more than you think," I suggested.

Fran gave me a hard look. "Would it matter? As long as I don't feel that they care, it doesn't do me any good. They're all on their own islands, as far as I can tell."

"How did it get this bad?" I asked.

Fran was lost in gloomy reflection. "Things fall apart. After we had been married for two years, Mitchell and I moved here, to a strange city. Phone calls home brought less comfort. Then when he dumped me, I was alone. Nobody wants to be around a woman when she's not part of a happy couple anymore. The invitations slow to a trickle, and then they stop coming," Fran said. "I went from being devastated to being depressed but coping. Now I'm actually used to it. There's still not enough oxygen in this house." She gave a curt laugh. "So now you know. I apologize for being so rough on you before."

She was drifting off again, becoming the woman who talked about herself as if she had long since moved away. Her mournfulness tugged at me, and I was almost pulled into it. But then I remembered.

"Fran, there was something here, and it was real," I said. I took both her hands in mine. "Tell me you felt it."

"I don't know," she said. "I never expected anything like this."

"Can I come back? Can we try again?"

She looked down without speaking, and I stood up. I folded the paper and put it into my pocket. "You have my number. If you don't call, that's fine. But we should be in touch," I said.

"If you want."

I left without saying anything more.

I walked in the long shadow of the row houses, which were too tightly spaced to allow cracks of light in between. The winter sun was sweeping quickly to the horizon. It disturbed me to leave Fran in a stricken state. She had thrown herself on my mercy; there was really no other way to put it. From the moment I'd asked her to name the people who truly cared about her, Fran's inner voice kept saying one thing over and over:

You're the only one I have.

It made no sense, and yet it made perfect sense. My heart still pumped when I thought about how close I had come to connecting with her. I had to be careful, though. She nursed all kinds of fantasies about being rescued, and I fit that slot too well. The important thing wasn't me; it was the presence that was in the room and that I didn't yet understand.

"The god of love is back," I murmured. My body continued to tingle with the energy that had streamed through it. Slowly my mind was coming to grips with a very peculiar possibility. I oriented myself and headed for home. Eventually, like a switch turning off, the energy disappeared. I felt drained.

When I got inside my apartment, I sank into the darkness of my living room and flipped on the television, then quickly turned it off again. I tried to reach Elena at her hotel, but the operator said she wasn't in her room. When my door buzzer sounded, I wasn't too surprised to find that it was her.

As she came in the door, Elena said, "I wanted to see how it went."

"You were there. How do you think it went?" I asked.

"Pretty well," she said, staring me straight in the face.

"I'm not so sure," I said. "Fran wasn't in great shape when I left. When I walked in, she was bitter and enraged. That's all she shows anybody. The pure victim, and I can't blame her. She feels worse now than when I showed up."

Elena seemed unmoved. "What happens next?" she asked.

"I told her I wanted to come back."

"We'll see how that goes. Fran might throw you out—when you push someone outside their limits, they rebound hard. She'll be more tense tomorrow than when you started." I was struck, not for the first time, by how Elena could read people with no more than a glance. Her only contact with Fran had been watching her across the street from a parked car.

Elena became philosophical. "Fran isn't alone. Most people crave love but behave as if they don't. She acts tough and vindictive, reciting a list of troubles over and over. That's all she thought she wanted you for, to be another earpiece."

"You don't think I'll get closer the next time?"

"You can't go in expecting to," Elena said. "Breakthroughs are personal and unpredictable. Consider them a kind of miracle that you might be privileged to observe but that you cannot cause. A miracle solves what looks to be impossible. Nothing feels more impossible than human suffering. We get trapped in it because we've lined up our unsolved problems like horses on a merry-go-round. Every day the same horses go around inside our heads. Old grievances, unforgotten pain, resentment, anger, failure, and insecurity—the circle keeps turning. Imagine a world that spins on an axis of suffering and no one can figure out how to stop it. Now you know what love is faced with every day."

"Then we have to do something," I said fervently. My body had become restless, and I was pacing while Elena stood in the middle of my living room with her coat on.

"I think I'll sit down," she said. She pushed a pile of newspapers off a chair and waited until I sat down, too.

"If love is real, don't you think it wants to save everyone?" she said gently. "How could it be called love if anyone is left to suffer?"

I hung my head. "Millions are left to suffer," I mumbled.

"There's no denying that. But millions are free to choose, also." Elena reached over and took my hand. "You're right, I was in the room with you—I'm not going to pretend about that. The subtle world connects everything. But I didn't create the power that you felt, and neither did you. It exists everywhere.

"I want to clear up something you thought was trivial—Dolly's task of having you pick up bricks. She wanted you to pick up each one with love. That's the only mystery and the only answer. Choose each moment with love, see each moment with love, feel each moment with love."

"If that's what she wants, then I can't do it. It's impossible," I said sadly.

Elena leaned very close. "Of course it's impossible. That's why they call it a mystery school. You must find the miracle that solves the impossible." Her face was glowing, and I felt a sense of awe, not at who she was, but at what was coming through her.

She regarded me with a gaze too deep for me to read. "There may only be a few of us who have broken through and who know the truth, but even we aren't responsible for what love accomplishes. We are devoted to it; we go where it guides us."

Did "us" include me? I didn't ask that question, and yet as still as Elena held herself at that moment, I thought she gave an imperceptible nod. "You're spooking me," I said, pulling my hand away.

"I know," she said. "It's inevitable, because there's a lot inside you that still doesn't want to accept any of this. If it's your time, though, and I'm sure it is, you will have glimpsed something incredibly important in that room with Fran today. Did you? Was there a message?"

I jumped to my feet. "You're making me very nervous," I said.

"I don't mean to."

I had to believe her, but the atmosphere seemed charged with expectation. "Does everything have to be a test!" I exclaimed.

"Pretty much." Elena smiled, inviting me into her relaxed, easy mood, but I clapped my hands over my ears.

"I don't want to hear it," I said.

"Then it's not for me to make you hear it." Elena said this without any sign of disappointment. "But be careful with Fran. Her situation is delicate and we need to respect that, even if she starts being afraid of you. You're the beast who jumped out of the bushes. In her mind the danger is that you know more about her than she does herself."

"But I don't," I insisted, feeling more disturbed as Elena talked.

"You know she feels empty. You know she wants to be rescued. You know that the love she wants and how she's trying to get it don't match. These are dangerous things to reveal to anyone." Elena got up, but I had come to a decision.

I pulled the wadded-up poster from my pocket and held it out.

"Ever since I met you, I've been telling myself that you're a mystic. Maybe I don't have the right word, but it never occurred to me that you were being literal. *The god of love is back.* That's not just some kind of metaphor?"

For the first time she looked taken aback. "No, it's not a metaphor. There is a god of love."

"How do you know he's back? Have you met him?"

She shook her head. "Dolly told me that she has. I think you have to if you're going to be the last wise woman."

"You asked me if I got a message while I was at Fran's apartment. I did. It said, *You don't have to look for love anymore. It's already looking for you.* Was that some kind of sign?"

"You might call it that. It's a piece of the truth. I don't know everything about everything." Elena gave a nervous laugh; she was still a bit thrown off.

"Was the god of love in that room?" I said.

"You'll have to discover that for yourself."

I allowed myself to smile. Elena's strategy, from the beginning, had been to give me glimpses of what I had to discover for myself. She was ready to leave, I could tell, so I offered to walk her out.

"No, you should stay." Elena came over to me. I thought she was going to kiss me good night. I leaned forward slightly, not enough to seem eager, just ready. Elena lifted her hand and rapped hard at my chest. It was the motion one uses to knock on a heavy door; I heard her knuckles strike my breastbone as the force of the blow shoved me backward. It hurt. In fact it hurt a surprising amount—I felt a squeezing pressure in my chest, and for a second the wind was knocked out of me.

"This is for desire," Elena said softly. There was a hint of seduction in her voice. But before I could react, she was out the door.

The pain kept growing, getting sharper and seeming to go deep, as if a blade was slowly probing its way inside me. I didn't cry out. But I released a loud gasp, and the sharpness of the pain vanished. I put my hand over the spot where she had struck me. The skin under my shirt felt warm. A few seconds later this faded, too.

I walked over to the window and watched Elena, who had come out the front door and was walking away. She crossed the street and became a distant figure in a black coat, a woman in the crowd on a Saturday night. She had been trying to make me see something about the mystery of life, yet more and more I wondered if the mystery wasn't Elena herself.

I almost expected her to leave a faint luminous trail in her wake.

This is for desire. I didn't miss the irony when Elena said those words and ran away. My mind dwelled on it as I undressed for bed that night.

Wasn't she constantly fending off my desire? I wouldn't blame you for accusing her of manipulating me. She threw mystification across my path at every turn. She never revealed any concrete facts about herself. Yet you'd be very wrong to think any of this mattered. Even if Elena had been as old and stooped as Dolly, I would have stuck it out.

Suppose that someone comes up to you on the street and says, "I believe you are yearning for a new life. I can show you how to find it." By turning your back, you can be rid of him. But then you have to consider: Who ever got a new life by turning away? Scorn is enough to drive away the charlatan, but it drives away truth, too. It's no secret that the material world is sorely lacking.

There was a phrase in the air: *Follow your bliss.* Where do people think they are following it to? What Elena called the radiance is where the bliss comes from. People who follow what they love will eventually get a glimpse of the radiance. They might stop there, of course. It's rare enough, God knows, to wake up one morning and be surprised by a sense of joy. But I don't think stopping at the threshold is the only possibility. Enough people will wonder, "How do I cross over?"

Which is why I found myself lying flat out on my bed staring up at the ceiling and thinking, *Bring it on.* I figured that when Elena hit me in the chest, she was opening a door.

I wasn't remotely sleepy when she left; it was barely seven o'clock. I ate some microwave spaghetti. I threw my garbage down the trash chute and took my laundry down to the coin machines in the basement. But I must have been too wired, because when I went to bed, sleep wouldn't come. At midnight, I was as awake as the minute I lay down. By three, my back hurt from rolling over in bed. I covered the clock and drew the blinds tighter. I found an old pair of swimmer's earplugs, which only made me hear the ringing in my head. The closest I came to dreaming was the sensation of being pressed under a heavy weight. I'd seen an etching like that in a book on medieval torture. My chest couldn't move, and a kind of slow-motion panic started to rise. I woke up thrashing. I tried rolling over, but my back hurt too much to stay in bed.

I padded around the apartment, then settled in the bay window and looked out over the bright patches of snow lingering on the rooftops. Because my eyes were used to the room's dimness, the whiteness swam in front of me and made the buildings seem close enough to touch.

"I know you're there," I murmured. I wasn't speaking to a person, but to the thing that lurked behind the scenery. I wondered if the sky ever opened up, if a seam parted and, as startled heads on the street craned to see, a huge face peered in from outside the envelope.

Around 8:15 I threw on my jacket and went outside. Sunday had come around again, and at least I could do what I always did. I got as far as my coffee place and stood by the door. Through the fogged window I spied couples sitting at tables, engrossed in conversations that stopped at the glass and became mute. It felt unreal. I half expected to press my finger into the side of the building and see it go through. Instead I kept on walking. Every once in a while I would look back over my shoulder, so strong was the feeling that crews were dismantling the scenery behind me, knocking down the paper-thin facade until I returned.

It took about twenty minutes to reach Boylston Street. The sun was out, and even though the sun was a cold winter sun, it magnetized a crowd. I slowed down to watch and listen. I'd be like a double agent in their world, a traitor who still knew how to blend in. I drifted north until my eye caught a woman buying a paper. She was just inside the door of a café, carrying a purple knapsack slung over one shoulder.

Renee. She was way out of her part of town here. She looked good. She tossed her head to keep the hair out of her eyes while she fished for change; she was smiling and chatting with the counter guy. She didn't feel me watching her, so I took my time crossing the street. She came out of the shop and turned left without noticing me.

I found that strange, but I was in the middle distance from her viewpoint. She could have missed me when a car came between us for a second. I followed her with my eyes. The feeling of desire gave me a suggestive nudge. I didn't anticipate it, but there it was. My eyes watched the sway of Renee's body as she strolled away. The throbbing place over my breastbone, which I'd forgotten,

came alive. It said, *What did you expect?* I ran and caught up with Renee. When I called her name, she turned around.

"Oh," she said, not "hello" or "hey." She hesitated a fraction of
a second before she smiled. This was enough to throw me off. She
remembered. She had been standing in my kitchen putting food in
the refrigerator, and she remembered the feeling of leaving without reassurance.

"I saw you buying your paper," I said to mark time. I wanted
Renee to give me an idea where to start. She nodded and her eyes
flicked up the street. "I didn't mean to startle you," I said.

"Are you out running?" she said absently, even though I wasn't
wearing my sweats and sneakers. I could have ignored this; I could
have invited myself to walk with her a while to see if she got a better feeling about me. But she might simply get worse, so instead I
told Renee how much I missed her. The nudge of desire pushed a
little harder; this opening might get somewhere.

"You just saw me a few days ago," she said, narrowing her eyes
slightly. She could see I was dancing around something I wanted
to say.

"I know, but we didn't get too far. I thought about calling you.
A number of times, actually. It kept slipping my mind," I said.

"There's someone else." The minute she said these words, Renee disliked my reaction. She wanted to go on, but I broke in.

"I shouldn't be surprised that you know," I blurted out. "But—"

"But what?" She was baffled. "You don't understand, Jess. I
mean I've found someone else. When I came over to your place, I
was going to tell you, but you were being so weird."

No thoughts hit me, so I said dumbly, "Who is he?"

"Somebody from work. Don't look at me that way."

"I'm not," I said. It didn't help that I'd already felt a crushing
weight on my chest in advance, and now it came back. Renee's

eyes were glancing up the street again. She was expecting him. I backed away. "Let's talk later," I said, hoping like hell not to set eyes on him. But Dolly's Law came into effect. When she told me that the story wanted to play itself out, she was really stating a cosmic rule: Every story wants to play itself out. A man's voice called Renee's name, and he came toward us. He was my age or thereabouts, well built with a big, ruddy face; he wore those glasses with the thinnest possible black wire frames that say, "I'm not really wearing glasses. This is an accoutrement." I hated him instantly.

He was introduced as Matthew, and he didn't say "Renee has told me so much about you, Jess." His expression showed no recognition at all. He stood with his arm around her shoulder, a shopping bag from the delicatessen dangling from his other arm. Renee became more relaxed; she wasn't in any hurry to get me on my way, and while Matthew told me something or other about the bear market, she met his glance instead of mine.

As soon as I could, I peeled off. I knew they weren't watching me leave. They were into each other; in five minutes they'd be in bed with bagels. The picture had to be wiped from my mind, although I could piece things together now.

She had come over to tell me about him because she assumed I would figure it out. First, there was the fact that she had been out of touch and hadn't asked if I wanted to be together for Thanksgiving. Second, there was the morning I woke her up too early. She'd gotten out of bed and carried the portable phone into the bathroom. Because someone else was in bed. A suspicious mind would have seized on these clues without waiting for a map.

No, that wasn't right. I had escaped from the lovers and gotten a couple of blocks away, far enough to calm down. The problem, the thing that was eating me, wasn't suspicion. It was a lie.

Renee had stopped being my girlfriend four months ago. I had let her go, offering a protest that registered on the scale from weak to zero. I'd keep loving her, I told myself. We would be more comfortable, in fact, because the mess of desiring each other—or not—would be gone.

Only, that was a lie. Love without desire is just another name for self-deception. The place where Elena hit me in the chest began to ache. I'd seen how Matthew's arm went around Renee's shoulder, his fingertips brushing the top of her breast. He was taking possession of his desire. He did it as if he wanted to emphasize that he had a right to. Of course he knew who I was—two men don't have to exchange cards—they *know*. His desire could flow into the empty place I'd left. Why shouldn't it? Desire flows constantly; it seeks its object when you're not noticing; it seeks when you're asleep. Matthew was nobody to me, but he was everybody who understood the one thing I'd missed. Love that denies desire is a lie.

My conscience was going biblical on me, driving a deeper ache into my chest. Who did I think I was? Renee had taken a chance on me by moving in, and then she felt the vacant place where I should have been. How long did it take her? Maybe not even a week. A man who couldn't—or wouldn't—satisfy a woman's desire to be loved was not what she wanted. She might have been hanging in there, hoping I'd wake up. I thought of how I called lovemaking "flopping the pillows." Most nights I'd ask her if she wanted to flop the pillows, and although she rarely said no, did Renee grimace inside? When I thought we were close, did she feel outside the circle I'd drawn around myself?

I kept torturing myself until a beat-up panhandler called out to me. He was stationed in front of a 7-Eleven, and I had ignored him when he shook his can under my nose. "I hope I never feel the way you look," he said in spite.

I had to get a grip. The thought of going back to my apartment was repugnant, but I had nowhere else to go. I went upstairs and paced. I couldn't call Elena. She was the last person, in fact. She was poison, the woman who wanted to show me the way to love everyone. Why had I bitten so fast? Because she kept my lie going. Dolly all but spelled it out. When we were shoved into the hall that first night, she said that Elena wouldn't ever fall in love with me. That should have driven me off; it only sealed my fate. I wasn't hanging around even though Elena was unavailable; I was hanging around *because* she was unavailable.

None of this was doing me any good. I tried the hotel and asked for Dolly this time, on the off chance that she had her own room. I had fantasies that she could absolve me in some way that only she knew. The operator said there was no Mrs. Feathering registered.

I made a decision and called Linny.

"What's going on? You don't sound right," she said when she heard my voice. There was no recrimination about the scene at Thanksgiving. I was relieved.

"I'm in a strange place," I said, telling her that a lot of things were hitting me all at once. I brought up Thanksgiving myself. "It's a crappy thing that happened. I'm sorry."

Linny hesitated. Between us, Elena and I had thrown her outside herself, but she had had enough time to get back. "Don't think a thing about it," she said, trying to keep the tone light. "You're my little brother. I was just worried."

"I'm not going to see that woman again," I said. "You know how ideas can seem good at the time."

"Sure, of course." The hint of nervousness that had been in Linny's voice was gone now. "It's not my place to say, but you're better off."

"I know." I waited to add another word of penance, to seal a pact with my sister. She wanted to be on my side; she wanted me to find a woman who would be good for me.

"They probably still have your old job waiting for you," she prompted. "You were good at it; they probably can't do without you."

"I don't know about that." My voice was getting weaker, but the pact was on the table. All I had to do was sign.

"Jess?"

"Sorry," I said. "I got distracted."

"Does that happen a lot? It's a sign of depression."

She shouldn't have said that. She shouldn't have opened the crack that let me see her real opinion. No man had ever turned to Linny and said, "Sorry I'm not here for you. I was contemplating a higher world." Because if he had, that was death. It would have sounded cruel and ludicrous to her. Men don't exist to feel love everywhere. She wanted love for herself, screw everywhere.

I didn't feel any more hesitation. "I have to run. I just wanted to know that you're okay," I said.

Linny sounded put off. "Josh takes good care of me, Jess."

I let it go and hung up. Lack of sleep caught up at last. I fell into bed and crashed until nearly sunset. Then I took the car down to the harbor. The gate to the vacant lot was padlocked. I looked in the backseat of my car and grabbed the navy pea jacket; the key I'd gotten from Elena was still in the pocket. With the construction crews gone, the neighborhood was quiet, except for the distant hum of traffic and the wind, which never dies this close to the water. I waited on the brick pile, pondering. I needed a new magic word. "My new life" wasn't working so well. It seemed fairly shot, in fact.

I looked up to see a cab pulling around the corner. Dolly got out and paid the driver. I got up to help her through the gate, but she waved me back to my seat. She had left her swathing of blue wool behind: her frizz of gray hair fluffed out in the wind as she tiptoed over the trash.

"Would you rather be seeing Elena?" she asked when she reached me.

"No, this is better, actually."

Dolly nodded. "You're wise. Self-pity is such an unbecoming state when you want to impress a young woman."

I wasn't in the mood for even gentle mockery, but then Dolly reached over and held her hand over mine. I knew something strong would happen. That had been the pattern, and this time was no different. My abdomen suddenly tightened into a knot; the pain came so fast that it took my breath away.

"There," Dolly said. She let go, and the tightness began to change, seeping out of my belly like oil through a crack. A cold numbness appeared at my fingertips and ran up my arms, then quickly into my trunk. It was the kind of sensation that overcomes you when you're deeply afraid.

When I could get the words out, I said, "Why did you do that?"

"To show you what you've been fighting against. It wasn't a phantom."

"What was it?"

Instead of answering, Dolly kept watching me closely. "If only you could pick up a brick."

"I can't, and I don't know why. Tell me that at least." But Dolly was in no mood to cooperate. She took a bony finger and drew a circle around my solar plexus.

"That's where you should be getting your power," she said. "But you can't if this place is empty. Emptiness has been your greatest fear and your strongest enemy." Whether her touch did it or not, I could feel a second wave of cold numbness settle in the pit of my stomach.

"Feel it now?" Dolly asked. "When the power place is empty,

you can't get what you want. There are no reserves to draw on. This is about more than a sensation, though." She sounded like a doctor diagnosing my pulse. "I can hear words coming from there."

Before I could ask what she meant, I heard them, too: *I wish. Please. If you don't mind.*

"Those aren't my words," I mumbled.

"Really? Then why do you feel so weak?" Dolly lifted my arm, and the muscles had turned to jelly. I tried squeezing my hands together—they couldn't have crushed an egg. The cold numbness in my stomach had sucked away my strength.

"Have you always seen this, looking at me?" I asked.

"Oh, yes." Dolly spoke with sympathy now. "When Elena and I are around, we give you a little injection—a boost—but on your own—" The sentence ended with a shrug. "This is where you lost your magic. *Please* and *I wish* are used when we depend on someone outside ourselves. If wishes were horses, every beggar would ride."

Her prim turn of speech would have been quaint, except that I was cringing inside, and when I tried to extract myself from that feeling, I couldn't. The cold numbness in my solar plexus sucked me back.

Dorothy nodded, following along with me. "The emptiness exists because you believe in it," she said. "You've adapted to having no power, but that isn't the condition in which you were meant to live. Give up what doesn't work and never will. Now listen." She raised her voice: "*I was born to the god of love. I will never beg again, not for the slightest thing.*" She eyed me sharply. "Do you believe that? Repeat it to yourself."

I tried, but the words sank into the hollow of my stomach and dissolved.

"Here," she said, touching me again. This time the coldness in my belly began to warm; the void began to fill.

I was born to the god of love. I will never beg again, not for the slightest thing.

The words felt more solid now, and I sensed something else. How can I describe it? Filling a pothole, patching a wire. These sound like clumsy comparisons, but that's what was happening. A hole was being filled, a link restored. But the hole was invisible, and so was what filled it. I got an image, though. I saw myself as a pale, lost boy, waiting for scraps of love like alms.

"Was that me?" I asked shakily. The image had been fleeting, but I was afraid of it.

Dolly nodded; her tone became serious. "You are experiencing what happens when you are cut off from your source. It's like a torn artery. Love is your life blood. It flows to support and nourish you everywhere. It courses through its own channels, not physically but in your awareness. If the channels are open, love brings all its gifts. You only have to send a request, and whatever you want will be yours. But if the lines are cut, love's power can't come through. You feel a void of desire. Not that you can quite name what you feel or put your finger on it. But the weakness is there all the same until you face it."

How can I put this to you without Dolly here? We're all haunted by the void. Time and again we test ourselves by running into some kind of battle or another. Maybe not armed conflict, yet its closest substitutes, the never-ending conflicts conjured up in everyday life. A woman you love loses faith in you, and you must find a way to restore it or admit defeat. A man you've betrayed has figured it out, and now you must repair that breach or lose him. You go inside to find out if you are harboring a void or something solid—something that will make you into what you want to be. Maybe it's a core of truth or faith or character. In Dolly's eyes, life can't be faced if the core is empty. With a touch, she had healed the void. Does this sound imaginary? Then tell me how else we can stop being beggars.

"See, that wasn't so hard," Dolly's eyes seemed to say. She wore a look of pleased satisfaction. Even so, a big part of me was reeling from the image of the pale, lost boy. Being humbled is a bitch. But I didn't have time for that—my belly was filling with a warm, liquid gold.

"Now maybe you'll become a man, yes?" Dolly saw me turn crimson and laughed. "Don't get mad. You've been a nice boy, and that boy can stick around as long as he wants."

She rushed on to cover my embarrassment. "You're lucky that it's only taken a week. Now you've experienced how powerful desire is. Without it, you will never ask love for enough."

"You'll stay a beggar," I said soberly.

"And go through life pretending you're not," Dolly said, finishing the thought. We sat in silence for a few moments.

The chill must have been making her frail frame ache; she was beginning to tremble. I quickly took off the pea jacket and threw it around her.

"Just a few more minutes," I said.

She gave me a tender look. "Don't you realize yet? I will deny you nothing," she said. The words sent a shiver down my spine. I had never heard such a thing from anyone since I was born, since those enchanted first years when a mother thinks them but we are too unformed to understand. It is mutely understood. Hearing Dolly say them made it seem as if being reborn could be real. Up to that moment the prospect of remaking myself was a concept. Now I heard the voice of love itself whispering, *I will deny you nothing*. Dolly was the conduit for a presence so all-encompassing that I couldn't grasp it without her—I hadn't gained enough power.

"What's it like?" I murmured. "To be you?"

Dolly couldn't or wouldn't answer. Instead she pulled an envelope out of her pocket. For a fleeting second I was afraid that a good-bye letter was inside. "It's the contract," she said. I couldn't read it in the dark, but I knew it was for renting the vacant lot.

"We put it in your name," Dolly added.

"Why?"

"Because you'll be in charge of the mystery school. And because the cops will hassle you without it."

I took Dolly's arm and helped her up. The buzzing arc lights that lit up the street went out for a moment, as they tend to do, and she became invisible, a piece of the night with wheezy breathing and soft, padding feet. Gingerly I led her out the gate. Her arm weighed little more than the empty sleeve of her coat. I was holding on to the last vestige of Nothing before it decides to return to its own world, which is All.

"I can't be in charge of the mystery school," I said. "You and I know that."

"Whoever shows up doesn't."

"So you want me to pretend?"

She didn't reply directly but said, "Don't beg for a thing. That includes answers." I led her around the corner. The streets were empty; I couldn't see a phone booth to call her a cab when suddenly one turned and came our way.

"You must be lucky," I said.

"You must be naive," she smiled. Dolly opened the back door of the taxi and hopped in without my help. She didn't wave or look back at me as she left.

I hadn't offered a ride because I still had one more stop to make myself. I felt great as I started driving. Camped out on the fringes of my life were truths waiting to be born. I had never figured out how to coax them in, yet now I could. The one possible ally in my new life was shaky. Very shaky, actually. I decided to go check on her.

When Fran answered the door, she had been given only a few minutes warning from a phone booth I found on the way. I expected to find her home on Sunday evening, and she was. I had asked if I could drop by to see how she was doing. Now she looked glad to see me. She pointed at two beers sitting on the coffee table. "They won't stain," she said. "Just in case." I sat down on the opposite sofa, just like the first day, to give her space.

"You want to know how I'm doing?" she said. "Nothing broken." Fran tilted her beer bottle, making a quick toast. She didn't want to seem afraid of me; that much was clear. "Maybe you can think up another game or whatever you called it," she volunteered. That was a surprise.

"I thought the last one made you unhappy."

"Maybe you won't believe this, but I didn't know I was so alone. When you have a lot of resentment, it fills up the room." She looked determined as she said this but not at ease. She was straining to look like she was back in control.

I said, "Are you expecting me to dig up more stuff?"

That earned a nervous laugh. "Maybe; I don't know."

"We don't have to talk about you at all," I said.

She looked relieved. "You're not drinking your beer."

"I can wait."

Fran shifted in her seat. I kept searching for a way to treat her as an ally. I didn't have a plan, only the beginning of an idea.

"I might have a new game," I said tentatively. "Do you want to hear it?" She nodded without answering. I felt tired, and if I waited, I was sure I'd give myself away. Obscurely, I knew I needed her as much as she needed me.

I said, "Imagine a girl who seems normal and happy, but when she's alone she has a fear that things aren't going to turn out well. When she grows up, she might not be pretty enough or smart enough. The boys who get interested in her could be the wrong boys.

"Yet in her fantasy it's all different. There, wonderful things happen; her life turns out to have magic in it. So she goes to her fantasy world as often as she can. Especially after the future turns against her. Pretty and smart are relative things, and so are boys. Nothing is perfect. Her worry anticipated all the problems she now had to face, but worrying did her no good dealing with them." I paused. "Do you feel all right about what I'm saying so far?"

Fran nodded; she was listening without tension. I already knew she was good at being detached. From time to time, she sipped her beer, yet she didn't look away.

"Eventually the girl became the kind of person she had never foreseen," I continued. "A realist. She settled, because that's what a realist does. Fate brought her a man who wanted her, even though he didn't match her fantasy image. After college everything accelerated much too fast, and there was no room for magic. But as hard as she tried to be realistic, settling didn't turn out well. Not the way she'd planned. Disaster struck."

Fran stopped paying attention. Her eyes had become flat. "I can stop," I said quietly. Fran looked uncertain. I was on the fine line between intimacy and invading her sanctum. I knew that I wasn't going to wound her. But she had to make the call about whether I should go on.

"I had an idea this was coming," she muttered. Her tone could be interpreted a dozen ways. It didn't sound that ominous to me, more like resigned.

"You can add anything you want to the story," I prompted.

She hesitated, then said, "The woman was pretending." I asked what she was pretending about. "Making people believe she was safe. Making herself believe." Fran sounded grim, and she added, "It was her own fault."

"I don't think so. That's guilt talking, and guilt always hides the truth."

I must have crossed the fine line between intimacy and intruding, because Fran suddenly bristled. "Are you speaking as God now?" She jumped to her feet and faced me down. "Or are you just my new protector? I've found a way to be safe. Why do you want to change that? Maybe you're a mistake."

"I'm not a mistake, but I won't deny I'm a risk."

"You're speaking to the wrong person about risk." I watched her begin to pace. I wasn't making her feel better, but that wasn't why I'd come.

"I'm only talking about this woman," I said. "We don't have to bring your name up at all."

Fran whipped around, hands on hips. "I liked you better when you were nervous," she said.

"Why?"

"Because it meant you were a bit afraid of me. Maybe you'll think I'm twisted, but I liked that."

"You're not twisted," I said. "You simply turned the tables from how you used to be. You get to be the strong one, even the aggressor now. You draw the boundaries and set the limits. Fine. But stop and think about it. Am I the right man to turn the tables on?"

I met her eyes. She was only going to be my ally if at some level she knew that we were connected. Elena had told me that my soul agreed to everything that was happening to me. This had to be true for Fran, too. I could see her backing off. She hadn't really been shaken by anything so far.

"This woman was knocked back hard," I said. "But after she got over being devastated and depressed and frightened—"

"And mad as hell," Fran interjected.

"Right, that too." My voice gained urgency. "After all her troubles, the woman knew for certain that she couldn't count on anyone. Nobody was going to love her deeply or unconditionally. No one would swoop down to rescue her. And being an extraordinary woman, far more so than she realized, she began to take comfort in this knowledge."

"She did?" Fran looked startled.

"Amazing as it may sound, she did. Because if she could admit that she was completely alone," I said, "her vision was clear, much clearer than before, when she depended on someone else. Now she was standing on her island with space and light all around, and although the view scared her, nobody was forcing any limits on her. She remembered the past, when she wanted magic; she remembered how those hopes died. Now they returned, but instead of being the magic a child dreams about, her desire was growing wiser."

"And she's stronger," Fran murmured.

"Strong enough that she isn't going to settle anymore. Nothing and nobody can kill her desire. It wants to take her into the unknown." I stopped to make sure that Fran was with me. Her face was glowing, and her eyes were fixed on me. "Her desire could walk through walls," I said, keeping my voice low. "It could visit secret lovers in the night and ask for the impossible. Does she want to follow where desire wants her to go?"

Fran didn't falter. "She has to. The unknown is the only place she can turn to." She didn't wait for me to take up the thread. "A voice inside says, *Change or die. Find a new way or you will be lost.* But that message is even scarier than being alone." I felt goose bumps. She had picked up the same voice I had been using. "So the woman tries to block the message out," Fran went on. "She doesn't want to believe. She's had more than her fill of risks."

I finished the thought, because it was mine, too. "Yet the

voice, faint and shy, keeps urging her. She must bring herself to trust in the unknown, because she doesn't want to die by slow degrees, does she?"

I stopped. We both knew we'd reached a turning point. Fran needed an ally as badly as I did. In some uncanny fashion we were both in the same place. Love and desire had become disconnected in us. I might have postponed this encounter forever, yet here it was. A woman whom I barely knew wanted something from my soul. Did she even know how much she was asking? At the moment Fran gave no sign.

"Do you believe what I just said?" I coaxed. It wasn't good enough to put her into a trance of hope; she had to step forward.

Fran took a deep breath and ran her fingers through her hair. "You almost had me," she said. "I always liked a sweet talker."

"It wasn't just talk," I said, still holding my breath.

"That's the sweet talker's second verse. Before he asks for the mortgage money." Fran gave a rueful laugh. The abrupt change in tone made the room feel empty, but I wasn't ready to give up.

"You don't have to sound so cynical about yourself," I said.

"I thought I was being cynical about you."

"It comes down to the same thing." I gave her a defiant stare. "Who else is in your life but me?"

She was startled. I wasn't sounding belligerent, but the grounds were there for taking offense. We both knew how empty her dance card was, only now I'd voiced it out loud, which is a different matter. "You can't force me to change," she exclaimed. "You shouldn't even be asking. It's not your place or your right. It's not—" Fran stopped herself; a wave of emotion was rising, and she had to concentrate to keep it down.

"Don't think about me," I said. "I'm not another man trampling your garden. Be alone, just for a moment. Close your eyes and see this woman we were talking about." With hesitancy, Fran slowly closed her eyes.

"This woman has to ask a big question now," I said, keeping my tone as even as I could. *"Where does love come from?* If it comes from other people, she's lost. She'll have to fight just to survive, alone as she is. But maybe love only comes *through* other people. Maybe they are the channel and not the source. Is that possible?"

"She doesn't know," Fran mumbled, keeping her eyes shut. Her voice was weak.

"I'll help her find out," I said. "But I won't do it for her. I can't."

Fran hung her head. She was shaken. When she sat down again, I moved beside her on the gray sofa. I put my arm lightly around her shoulder, just enough so that she would know I was there. She flinched at first, then she rolled her body into the crook of my arm. For a second I wondered how it had all gotten this far and what would happen next. I put my other arm around and held her. She nestled closer and lay still.

"I can't stop being a woman," she whispered.

"That's good enough for me."

After a while Fran sat up; she managed a tired laugh. "I'm such a mess." Her body was off balance, and as she struggled to her feet she wobbled and had to sit down again. "Don't agree with that," she warned. "And don't disagree either. Do you have to go?"

I shook my head. "What made you think that?"

"I guess a few men made me think that." But the old harshness in her voice didn't return. She sighed deeply. "You used one word back there—*realistic*. That's me, and I'm going to disappoint you if you don't know that."

"I'm realistic, too," I said.

"Are you?" Fran gave me a searching look. "You're sure you're not a silver-tongued devil? You might be deceiving both of us."

I laughed. "You could be right. I never know if I'm making this up as I go along."

I meant the remark to be disarming, but Fran's mouth shaped itself in a thin, straight line—it had looked like that when she warned me on the street not to break into her house.

"I didn't mean it that way," I said. Fran nodded doubtfully. But her mood shift wasn't fatal, and after a moment she relaxed again.

I said, "It's time I told you who I am."

She wanted that, but she was also starving, as it turns out. My first visit had taken away her appetite for almost a day. We wound up going to a restaurant she knew. I kept quiet as we walked. Fran needed time to decompress, and so did I. I was happy, though, almost sublimely happy, compared to a few hours before. I was going to trust in the unknown. You might think I was opening my arms to embrace the night, but the unknown wasn't dark or empty or frightening. Something amazingly potent lived there. It watched me, it knew me, it understood what needed to happen. I myself had no idea what needed to happen, but I'd caught a whisper from the unknown: *I will deny you nothing.*

I WOKE UP the next morning with a mystery school to attend. Two days ago, the vacant lot was a rubble pile where Dolly had had me playing a pointless game. Now I couldn't wait to get back there and find out what the mystery wanted to say today. Did I already mention that every day was like a different world? This one was going to be the best yet—I had received a portent.

During the night, I was revisited by the sensation of liquid gold filling my body. When Dolly touched me, the sensation was confined in my solar plexus, but this time it streamed everywhere. I couldn't tell if I was awake or asleep. I kept wanting to open my eyes, but I had no strength to move, even though I felt wide awake inside. I could think; I could even remember, as the gold seeped into each finger and up through my chest, something I'd told Fran: Trust the unknown. What I hadn't known was how incredibly sweet the unknown becomes when it bursts like a warm peach in your mouth. No one can describe it, just as no one can describe the scent of damask roses or the luster of pearls. Yet as I lay there, the sensation of molten light was beyond all of these. I had no sense of time, but I think it was only a matter of minutes before everything faded to black.

The memory was still alive in the morning, and I felt an urgency that wouldn't be denied: *Bring it back.* If I could have that same sensation twice, why stop there? I threw on some clothes and ignored breakfast. Driving down to the harbor, all I could think about was what would happen next.

Impatience wasn't rewarded. I sat on the rubble pile under gray skies threatening to drop rain, sleet, or snow, depending on what blew in from the sea. The demolition crew in the next block had returned, so the din around me was terrific. A few people walked by the open gate. I was bursting to grab the next willing stranger. Everybody needed to know what I knew, but none of them lifted their heads.

I figured I had to jump-start things. Maybe I should keep doing what Dolly told me, so I ran in place until I could feel my legs again. I imagined her wrapped in her blue scarf expecting me to find one perfect brick. But I couldn't get motivated. I kept looking at the ugly, shapeless mass. Then I knew why nothing was happening. I was in the wrong place.

I got in my car and headed back downtown. In five minutes I was pulling up in front of the hotel, just in time to see a bellman loading luggage into a limo. Behind him stood Dolly and Elena. When they saw it was me, neither seemed surprised.

"You're leaving?" I said, trying not to sound as disturbed as I felt. "Why didn't you call?"

"You got up early. When we called, you'd already gone," Elena said. She was in her long, black coat and was holding Dolly's arm. The old lady looked particularly frail with the sharp wind stirring her frizz of hair like tangled cobwebs. Her eyes were dull and didn't meet mine. I was sure something was wrong.

Elena had no trouble reading me. "She just needs to be at home. We'll have you up as soon as we can." Seeing that the bags were loaded, she helped Dolly into the backseat, then turned to face me. "Don't regard this as good-bye."

"How should I regard it?" They had made a wrenching decision without me, and Elena was communicating in bite-sized sentences. What was I supposed to think?

"Don't worry about us. Just go back. The right things are happening," Elena said. Her voice sounded kind but detached—she seemed to have a whole repertoire of detachment.

"How come every time you reassure me, I wind up feeling left out in the cold?" I said. I was being pretty literal, given the time I'd been spending down by the water by myself.

"Just because there's something for Dolly and me to do alone doesn't mean we left you out." Without another word, Elena slipped into the backseat, and the door shut. They drove away behind smoked glass.

I couldn't find any better course of action than to return to the vacant lot, though it didn't feel like the right place when I got there. It felt like the only choice, when no choice makes sense. Instead of sitting on the rubble heap, I leaned against the chain-link fence and waited. The noon hour came and went. The demolition crews stopped their clanking and banging, then started it up again.

"What are you doing?"

I turned around. A woman had been driving by in a black sedan and was stopped at the curb. She leaned out the window, removing her wraparound sunglasses. "What's that you're doing?" she repeated louder, in case the noise had drowned her out the first time.

"I'm looking for a brick."

"Is that a joke?" The woman, who was around forty, got out of her car. "I'm Gloria," she said. That was all the introduction she felt was necessary. She was Fran's type, I thought to myself, meaning one of the urban restless. But she wasn't as discontented looking as Fran, and she hadn't let her weight go. I'm not painting a flattering picture because her immediate vibe was too bossy—it was the vibe of a woman who kept score.

Gloria pointed at a brick. "How about that one?"

"It's not that easy," I said.

"Maybe it's easier for me because I don't know what you're doing." She came through the gate and took a seat on the rusty bed frame. "I hope I don't get tetanus."

Here's my willing stranger, I thought grimly, the one I was bursting to embrace. But Gloria didn't look all that willing. Then a thought hit me.

"Are you here to check me out?" I said.

"Basically." She apparently saw no reason to beat around the bush. Instead of asking her why I needed checking out, I put two and two together. Gloria must be Fran's best friend, the one on the phone who had more trouble with men than Fran. To hide my annoyance, I went back to staring at the rubble. Gloria watched mutely. I tried to detach myself from her opinion, which couldn't have been good. It seemed kind of pointless to be watched doing nothing, so I picked up a brick and almost immediately threw it back.

"What was wrong with that one?"

I had no reason not to tell her. "This is an exercise. It's kind of like Zen. I'm teaching myself how to choose. If I feel tense, the choice isn't right. If I'm angry or resentful, it isn't right. If I feel self-doubt or distracted, it isn't right."

"There are a lot of ways not to be right," she commented.

"The list gets longer, believe me." Gloria looked blank, so I didn't tell her that maybe she could learn something herself. My warm core of love was growing as cold as my freezing backside, which had gotten soaked sitting on the damp rubble. "Maybe you think this is stupid, but it might have a higher purpose," I pointed out.

"You wish." Gloria laughed and put her wraparound glasses back on. "I shouldn't make fun of you. You must be some kind of saint in training, right?"

She was challenging me to prove I was sincerely into my nonsense. I picked up a brick and quickly put it down again.

"You rushed that one, I saw you. And you were distracted by me," she said amiably. "I think I'm catching on." The muscles at the base of my neck started to bunch. Gloria pointed to a brick with a white corner sticking out near my head. "That one. Give it a try."

Okay, I could be tolerant. A saint in training has to be. I took a step up, making sure the debris didn't shift under my feet, and grabbed the brick. There was a folded piece of paper underneath. I opened it up, feeling strange. It read, "Congratulations."

I turned in amazement. "How did you do that?" But Gloria wasn't good at keeping a straight face. "Thanks," I said drily, seeing her grin. I tossed the paper away.

"I saw you a couple of days ago, so I planted the note," she said. "I thought you'd think it was funny."

"Good hunch. We don't want me to take this whole thing too seriously." I climbed down and kicked at the rubble as if my boots needed cleaning. "Is Fran meeting you here? She'll be sorry she missed the payoff."

"Who's Fran?" Gloria looked genuinely puzzled.

"Forget it, I'm going home," I said.

Gloria put her hand on my shoulder. "I wouldn't do that, Jess. Who would mind the school?" She laughed again, this time not at me. "Dolly never told me you were this easy to embarrass. But the note's not a joke. You can stop now. There's something else going on."

"What is it?" My mind had already flashed that this was no friend of Fran's, but that was old news by now. "Were you sent to give me a message?"

Gloria didn't reply. Her gaze surveyed the vacant lot. She seemed to love what she saw as much as Dolly and Elena had. "I wanted to see for myself," she murmured. "It's a big step for us. How did you ever get them to do it?"

"I didn't get them to do anything." When she said "us" I felt almost sick to my stomach. It had never occurred to me that there was anybody but Dolly and Elena and me. "I don't get it," I stammered. "Who are you? Why did you show up now?"

Gloria smiled indulgently. Her face grew softer, although she was the furthest type I could imagine from a . . .

My mind ran into a barrier. What would you call the three of them? Suddenly Dolly and Elena were no longer unique. They belonged to a class of something unnameable.

Gloria had no more trouble at reading me than the others. "We're devotees. We worship the god of love." Hearing these words in a clipped accent from a woman wearing sunglasses on a cloudy day did not compute. "You're having an image problem," Gloria said tolerantly. She put her hands together and rolled her eyes to heaven. "Better?"

"No."

"I guess you think love has to be squishy? I'm little too savvy for that."

She wasn't twisting things all that much. I thought love had to be tender, and in feminine form, soft and yielding. If that bothers you, then enjoy my comeuppance, because Gloria had none of Elena's mystique or Dolly's frailty. I'd given up the fantasy that I was their rescuer, but hadn't I stumbled into a private world? A world that took me in, and me alone?

"It can't be a private world," Gloria said soberly. "It's a world where anyone can enter. You don't have to fit an image. You just have to honor *what is*." It had been a long time since Dolly had used that phrase. It was hard to understand when she said it, and now even more so from Gloria.

"You don't have to look so disappointed," she said. "You're part of something you haven't fully grasped." Gloria had on thick winter boots, and now one foot kicked aside a patch of bricks, maybe five or six lying together. She spotted a crushed weed, now a flattened clump of dead leaves. Kneeling down, she fondled it carefully, as if coaxing it back to life. I couldn't see anything happening, then Gloria glanced up and said, "Careful behind your foot there."

I followed her eyes. Behind me, a small cluster of greenery stood out from the frozen ground, and on a dangling stem hung a miniature orchid. It was white with a speckled purple throat, like those that grow in meadows deep in the woods.

"We never had orchids that I can remember," Gloria murmured. "I think they were asphodels. I'm more the asphodel type." This was such a ludicrous remark that she must have made herself laugh.

"How did you do that?" I said. This wasn't the first time I'd seen winter turn to spring, but she seemed to be like the mechanic who knew how the apparatus worked.

"I move the energy," she said. "It's not like other energy you know about. It's alive, for one thing, and anyone can tap into it."

"Where do you tap it from?"

"Everywhere. You don't have to meter it out. There's never less life energy, or more. It's the core of *what is*."

"So you could use it to transform anything you wanted?"

"Even you." Gloria flashed me a wicked smile. "But I can see Elena's been doing a little makeover already. She's got a gentler touch."

Things were moving too fast. I said, "Stop throwing new stuff at me for just one moment. I still don't know why you're here."

"That all depends on you." Gloria eyed me steadily. "It's okay to be greedy, but it's better to stay the course."

"I don't know what you're talking about."

"I'm talking about last night. You had a first taste of nectar, didn't you?"

I didn't jump. I was past being startled, but giving up my private world so fast was deeply disturbing. *All right, let's assume she knows everything.* I said, "Having a taste doesn't make me greedy. Wouldn't anyone want more? I thought that was the whole teaching—follow your desire."

"If we had all the time in the world, you could follow your desire. We all remember our first taste; it haunts us. For years we chase it. It becomes our chimera, our unicorn. What's mythical to others is so real for us that by comparison everything else tastes like dust." Unexpectedly Gloria's voice drifted off into the same dreaminess that occasionally overcame Elena. Just as suddenly she came back. "But this is different. We're coming out into the world, and you're the only one who knows."

I looked down at the tiny orchid surrounded by rubble. Despite the winter wind, it nodded without withering or freezing. I'd had time to start adjusting to Gloria. Enough time to realize that Dolly and Elena, if they weren't unique, must also not be the only ones in hiding. The pang I felt at losing them for myself wasn't gone, though.

"I need to talk to all of you," I said.

"In time you will." Gloria saw my hesitation. "Don't blame us for leading you on. Dolly and Elena both love you, but their life is not . . ." She paused to find the right word. "Negotiable."

"You mean their purpose comes first?" I said.

Gloria nodded. "Close your eyes. I want to show you something."

I did, and unlike the time with Elena when I saw the peasant girl in the field, this image came instantly, in sharp detail. My nose was filled with the heavy resin smell of pines. The shadows of tall trees held perfectly still all around me. I knew immediately that I was in a sacred grove, so removed from the world that even natural sounds couldn't penetrate. No birds sang or creatures rustled. But what held my gaze were the women—a circle of priestesses in white robes. Their faces were pale and beautiful. Each one knew I was there, because their eyes solemnly met mine. I could tell I wasn't an intruder, but my role was unclear. I felt an urge to enter the sacred circle. First I wanted one of the priestesses to give me permission. Were we in Greece or some Arcadia known only in myth?

"That's enough," Gloria said softly. When I opened my eyes, she asked, "Can you remember what you just saw?"

I nodded, still flooded by the sensation. "The women were all looking at me. But I couldn't recognize any faces," I said, having a hard time shaking off my sense of being held in their gaze. The effect was so powerful that I hadn't broken my eyes away to search for Elena. If I had found her—or Dolly in some guise—maybe I would have finally understood who she really was.

"Listen carefully," said Gloria. "That image is one you've been carrying around this whole time. It's not real. It's not us. If it ever was, this world will never allow it back. I don't want to bruise your fantasy, but give it up. We aren't sacred virgins communing in a grove."

I opened my mouth to ask if everything was a prank with her. But Gloria didn't look like she was mocking me. She was quietly serious. I held myself in check, and she said, "If you want to run after the golden juice, go ahead. This is business, though, the kind that's going to change everything."

She was certainly a smart tactician. Seeing my fantasy fleshed out made it seem trite and flimsy, and I began to let it go. It was harder to give up the golden juice, but I wanted to stick with anyone who sounded so certain about accomplishing the impossible. Just as instantly, however, the spell broke. "Wait," I said. "There's no way you need me, and there's no way I make the difference whether you come out of hiding."

I don't know if I caught her off guard or if she was afraid I was about to rebel, but Gloria suddenly decided to change tactics. "Come with me," she said.

Gloria turned on her heels and headed out the gate. The abandoned block where the vacant lot stood wasn't remote. After we rounded the corner and walked a couple of blocks, we reached a busy thoroughfare. The threat of rain and sleet had passed, and the cloud cover was quilted with thin shafts of light.

"We can stop here," Gloria said. "I want you to observe." There was mostly car traffic on the street, but it was getting to be near rush hour, and a lot of pedestrians passed us. Not knowing what to look for, I took them in. It wasn't a Yankee parade or even an Irish-Italian one. Boston has grown a lot more ethnic over the last decade—many black and Asian faces appeared and various accents of Spanish.

Gloria didn't quiz me on any of what I was seeing. "Can you

tell me which person on this street is most like you?" she said. Before I could answer, she pointed to a ten-year-old girl walking in the middle of a noisy family group; she was shouting to get her mother's attention. Gloria pressed my shoulder to keep me from commenting. "Now let's find some who are the most unlike you." She didn't point out one individual this time. Instead her arm swept in the scene. "Basically the whole street." She hesitated. "With apologies to that Chinese grandmother over there. I was a little too quick."

"All right," I said. "Assume you've totally mystified me. What are you seeing?"

"I'm looking at how people use their energy. See that woman on the corner, the one with the baby in her arms? She's spending a lot of energy worrying about how to manage her time. Another portion goes to resenting the father, who won't do his share, and being afraid of the future. That man in the gray suit, the one buzzing himself into the ATM. He's exhausted. He spent almost all his energy at work.

"I look around and a precious resource is being squandered. Almost everyone has left pieces of themselves scattered behind, or else they focus on externals that will contribute very little to happiness in the long run."

She kept showing me the play of energy around us, pointing out a girl who Gloria said was flashing brightly because she was meeting her boyfriend, and an old man who she said was like a depleted battery with almost no reserves left. "Maybe you find it strange, but I see bundles of life energy walking the streets, churning and churning. Do you know why I'm so disturbed?"

"Because it's the same energy you used back there to make an orchid appear," I said slowly. The conclusion came easily, because Gloria knew what she was doing. She had built her case bit by bit, weaning me from fantasy and greed to this moment.

I tried to see as she was seeing. The crowd continued to pass, and maybe I did catch glimpses. Of gray shadows around some people and not around others. Of flickering sparks in a few people or a faint shimmer. I shook my head, and Gloria said, "It's all wrong. You probably jumped to a conclusion about me. You think I'm cold-blooded and objective. But I have a passion to change people. I'm the strongest voice for coming out into the world, because all this waste of energy can be changed."

To prove her point, she began to teach me: "There are three centers to observe when you want to truly know a person: the head, the heart, and the solar plexus. As life energy comes into us, it divides into thousands of tiny channels, but these three are the main portals. The solar plexus is a reservoir of power, the heart is a reservoir of emotion and sensation, the head is a reservoir of vision and creativity. The amount of energy you can take in and use determines how your life turns out. Potentially there should be a balance of power, feeling, and vision. When balance exists, a person is relating to the universe in a natural way. Desires arise, one sees how to fulfill them, and the fulfillment brings increased joy."

I couldn't fully see what Gloria saw, but I knew people who had more heart than power or more vision than heart. I knew men who drove themselves to succeed without gaining any real knowledge of life or compassion for others. At the opposite extreme, I knew women who loved deeply but seemed to have no power to run their own lives or who felt devoid of a vision to guide them.

"Show me someone who's in balance," I said.

"That little girl I pointed out to you was the only example I saw," Gloria said. "But you are getting there. Dolly and Elena have been working on your centers. Compared to the day you met them, you have much more vision, feeling, and power."

"Is that always part of your work?"

"Yes, because it's the work of love. Love brings perfect balance when it is allowed to flow freely. Life energy always contains love. Therefore I care only if someone's energy is being used as love intends—to bring fulfillment. People analyze their lives a million other ways. Rarely, though, does anyone stand back to ask the simplest question: Am I using my share of energy to bring myself the deepest fulfillment? This question is more basic than how you behave or earn a living or relate to others. Your soul sent you away from the subtle world to find your fulfillment here."

"Why leave the subtle world at all?" I asked.

"Because your soul doesn't experience love. It *is* love. You might compare this to having immense artistic talent. Would a great painter be content to have enormous potential but never put brush to canvas? The soul is love, yet without being born it can't express love. You are the vehicle for its expression, using your energy to create each day as perfectly as you can."

"Then why don't people know that?"

"They're distracted. When your soul cuts you loose and sends you here, the dramas you can participate in are countless. Nobody escapes the fascination. Why should they? A million dramas won't exhaust even the tiniest fraction of all the life energy there is to go around. Take an infinite amount away, and there will be an infinite amount left over."

"Was I any different? I was pretty distracted," I said.

For a second Gloria looked as if she was going to say, "God knows." Instead she decided to tell me part of her own story. "I was a street kid raised in the inner city. By the time I was ten, I was a savvy customer, and no one could tell me what to do. I got what I wanted by hook or by crook, including a car by the time I was fifteen. One night I crashed the car—it doesn't matter how—and wound up in the hospital. There were enough brothers and sisters at home that my mother couldn't come to see me except an hour a day, and my father only made it in after work.

"Being stuck in a hospital bed when you're a teenager is torture. With nothing to do, I became curious about the old woman in the next bed. She was gaunt with illness, and although I knew she must be dying, I wasn't afraid. Death had no meaning at my age, anyway. Whenever visitors came, they always drew the curtain around her bed, so all I heard was murmurings. But I'd never seen such a genteel old lady. She sprinkled lavender water on her hands every morning, and if she knew a visitor was coming, she did her hair and had a nurse prop her upright in bed.

"She never asked me about myself, and since I was only going to be there for two days, I didn't go out of my way to get to know her. She just struck me as quiet and peaceful for somebody who might not live out the week.

"The night before I was going home, I couldn't sleep. The nurse had given me a pill, but I'd flushed it down the toilet. All I wanted to do was get back on the street the minute they'd let me. I dozed off around two in the morning, only to wake up with a start. The room was dark but I saw the old lady standing over me. I would have screamed if I hadn't recognized it was her. She hadn't been able to get out of bed the whole time, but there she was, looking down at me without a word.

"I asked her if I could help her get to the bathroom or something. She shook her head. It was spooky, so I asked her what she was doing. She said, 'If you're not careful, you'll destroy yourself.' Her voice was clear and strong; that alone would have freaked me out. I didn't know what to say, so I told her to go back to her bed. 'Not until we do a little rearranging,' she said, which doubly freaked me.

"I couldn't find the nurse's button in the dark, so I lay there praying she wasn't crazy enough to hurt me. In fact she didn't do a thing. After a moment she turned away and went back to bed. When I left the next morning, she was still asleep with her face turned away so the light wouldn't wake her up. Unpacking my bag at home I found a small envelope. Inside was a note that smelled of lavender. It said, *I will be dead when you read this note. Forgive me for disturbing you—a mother should never frighten her children.*

"That note changed my life. I called the hospital, and in fact the old lady had passed away an hour after I checked out.

"Why did this happen to me? I can't do the cosmic math that brought me into contact with Miss Sophia at that moment. It was just my time, and in her dying moment she knew it."

Miss Sophia was the last wise woman before Dolly. I could see that Gloria was feeling a lot from recalling her memories. I asked her how she found out who the old lady was. "The thread wasn't picked up until fifteen years later. I was up in New Hampshire and had stopped at a gas station. Dolly was sitting in the next lane while her husband was filling up their car. She rolled down her window and quoted Miss Sophia's note. I'm sure you know how it went from there."

I was very glad to hear the story—it brought Gloria into the company of Elena and Dolly so that I could accept her. "So everyone has to stumble into their own awakening," I said.

"You missed part of the story," Gloria said. "Miss Sophia was changing my energy that night. She could see what I've now learned to see myself, and what you will see very soon. People's lives are changed only when their energy changes. If they don't know how to do it, we should step in. That's why we have to come out into the world." Gloria sounded fervent when she told me that a lot of the group agreed with her.

This implied a number beyond the three I knew about. "How many are there?" I said.

"Come with me and find out. You look ready to accept who we

are. If you told us we could be sacred priestesses in the woods, we'd laugh. We don't care about more dramas, even sacred ones. Like you, we want nectar. We crave the pure essence. And the only way to get the pure essence is to leave the husk behind."

Suddenly the story was back to me and what I was supposed to do. "Is that where Dolly and Elena went, to be with the group?"

"Yes. And you should come, too, if you belong." Before I could ask her how I would know, she said, "You have to be like a minstrel at the palace who steals away by night. The king may beg you to stay; he may offer you the hand of a royal princess if only you'll keep playing. But you're a minstrel, and you must refuse, because without the road ahead, there is no music."

Gloria stopped. We were standing on the curb next to traffic. Every time the light changed, another surge of restless moving bodies swept around us. But she wasn't really there, the way Dolly and Elena weren't really there. I guessed she had come to check me out because nobody except Dolly and Elena believed I should be let inside their group, whatever it was called. In fact, this seemed the right moment to ask. "What do you call yourselves?" I said.

"The daughters of joy," said Gloria. "It's not official. We don't have a letterhead or a secret handshake. But we all got where we are by turning our sorrow to joy, so the name fits."

Suddenly she became restless. "I don't want to stand around here anymore. Nobody cares enough about the mystery. They don't know what their lives are trying to say."

"*I will deny you nothing,*" I muttered.

She couldn't disguise her surprise. "So you're not clueless. Good, I didn't want to have to push you into traffic."

I laughed and began to feel great, then better than great.

Remember when we started, I mentioned that the universe has

a sense of humor? Just look at me. I was breathing bus fumes on a nasty day in Boston. This savvy customer who could probably rebuild a carburetor was giving me the cosmic lowdown. Unbelievably, absurdly, divinely, it really was my time. I was a blind caterpillar at the tip of a banana leaf. I had been on solid ground with every step I crawled. Now the last one, another half inch, would end in deep space. The fact was as obvious as my haircut or my shoes. A thousand things I haven't told you about my life suddenly fell into place. The effect was like a velvet explosion going off in my chest, not the liquid gold of the night before but a blast outward that knew no bounds. It was like being in on the cosmic joke and getting to run with it.

Gloria noticed. "Don't bliss out on me," she warned, grabbing my arm and pulling me down the street. "We need you." By the time we reached the vacant lot again, the wind had turned from the sea and brought cold rain falling in stinging pellets. I pointed to my car, and we dove inside. I was grinning like a banshee while trembling from head to toe.

"You're looking kind of shaky," Gloria said. "Can we depend on you?"

To be honest, I wished the question would go away. I felt the beginning of another wave of sweet bliss, and I wanted it to be my own. I hadn't known how much I craved this moment. But I fended off greed long enough to mumble, "What happens to me if I go with you?"

"What you've been waiting for all this time." Gloria leaned close to make sure I heard her. "You get to live the mystery."

THE ROADS to New Hampshire had been swept clean of snow by all the recent rain. The last thing Gloria told me was that the daughters of joy would meet at Dolly's. That was in three days' time, but I decided to go immediately. Boston looked faceless and gray in the predawn light. Fran was asleep beside me in the front seat. She didn't know why I was dragging her up there. It wasn't something I could tell her. But in a way I had no choice; we seemed to be tied together.

I showed up on her doorstep soon after Gloria drove away. It was six o'clock and already dark. I phoned ahead, but Fran was fumbling with the sash of her bathrobe when she answered the door. "I'm not very together," she mumbled. She led me into the living room where the TV was going.

"I just have to catch this last bit," she said. We sat through a few minutes of some police drama. It was pretty obvious that she'd had a setback.

She clicked the remote and said, "Mitchell called. He wants us to get back together. We talked a long time."

I didn't raise my eyebrows, but Fran reacted as if I had.

"I know what you're thinking," she said. "But don't worry, I still hate him, and I didn't commit to anything." She tried to keep her voice flat and detached despite the turmoil inside. "I know what you're thinking," she repeated, this time more doubtfully. "But I've got to make up my own mind." Fran ducked her head like a fist-fighter on the defensive. It was hard to look at her.

I had raced over on a high, wanting to spread some joy, I guess. My body was still vibrating, but the minute I saw Fran the crystal cracked. I searched for a reply. "If you do anything he says, you'll get in trouble."

"I already told you that, didn't I?" Fran jumped to her feet. She was wearing those puffy slippers that make you look like you're stepping on a rabbit. "I didn't call you earlier because you'd only throw it back at me." I listened while she poured out the rest: Mitchell had broken up with the woman he left Fran for, and his business was suffering. Fran had tried to push him away, but old feelings had come flooding back when she heard his voice. Mitchell told her that he knew her better than anyone else ever could. Fran was touched. Then he cried. Did that mean they were soul mates or just addicted to each other?

Letting her talk gave me time. There had to be a reason why I was there. My eyes drifted toward the window, where raindrops made silvery trails running down the glass. I heard the wind's eerie moan in the heating ducts.

"I don't need you to help me; I'm going to do what I have to do," Fran said. She kept me in a hard stare and then reminded me about something I had told her—that she should trust the unknown. She had no concept what that meant, she admitted, but she had tried. And what happened? An amorous, half-drunk ex-husband had woken her up at three in the morning and turned everything upside down. It was like climbing out of a deep pit and at the brink, when you think you've made it, a hand reaches out of the dirt to drag you down again.

Her voice began to fade, and very softly I disappeared. All the conflicts and differences melted away, and I felt that everything was going to be all right. One minute I was in a room trying to solve a problem I knew I couldn't solve, and then my next heartbeat was on the threshold of eternity. They erased the name from my birth certificate and my tombstone at the same time. No more Jess. He ran down the window with the raindrops, leaving a faint, silvery trail. It was like reaching zero, and maybe that scares you. In reality it felt like the end of everything scary, because what I touched wasn't zero. It was purity.

"You're beautiful, and you deserve everything that's good," I said. My voice was clear and strong as it cut through Fran's bitter complaining.

She looked at me like I was deranged. I didn't return the gaze. A part of me thought I was deranged, too, not because of what I'd just said. Because I meant it for *everyone.* I snatched the remote and clicked on the TV again. I flipped until I found CNN.

"Look," I said, my voice still clear and strong. "For one minute just look."

She thought I was shutting her down, but she looked anyway. Dolly's favorite program was on: war, famine, outbreaks of violence, and horror. For the first time, I could see it the way she did. I could see that everyone was just the same. They were dealing with stuff that tore their lives apart, but underneath, nobody was moving. They were just marking time.

Fran didn't know how to react. "Say something," she snapped.

I pointed at the screen, which was showing some mob scene with police clubs and tear gas. "They're like you. They're waiting to find out something. Until they do, they won't stop raging. Their despair keeps driving them, as well as their anger and a sense that nobody will ever rescue them."

Fran hadn't got past the first three words. *"Like me?"* She screeched pretty close to my ear, but it didn't bother me, since I had disappeared. The mystery had walked past my door and brushed me with its skirts. Fran looked furious when I began to smile. But I held out my hand as if grabbing the end of a thread. I tugged at an invisible tangle, and it came undone. The tangle had covered her heart; I put my hand in the air near her chest and swept away a gray shroud. Her heart was still obscured, and the tangle was still coming undone, but I could see light begin to glimmer.

If Fran had jumped back, I would have stopped. If she had told me I was crazy, I would have let her throw me out. Neither happened. Her eyes closed and her face completely relaxed. She swayed gently on her feet; I helped her sit down on the sofa. I was laughing softly now. Fran didn't react because she had slipped into a light doze. Anyway, she wouldn't have caught on. I was remembering that first night at Dolly's when I had dozed off. It's funny what a canny old lady can slip past you.

As Fran slept, I watched her energy. She wasn't in good shape yet. I noticed jags and tears that looked like black streaks in the light that surrounded her. Those must be the most wounded parts. Some of the blackness was old; I could feel their hard, stubborn power over her. There was a murky cloud around her head, but no part of her body was bright—the congestion of her misery had made it nearly impossible for new energy to come in or old energy to leave. All of this could be changed, though. I didn't even have to move my hands; it was enough to see what was wrong and ask inwardly that it be removed. Gradually the whole field around her became lighter. I watched and waited.

Things have been moving so fast here that I didn't tell you what everyone on CNN was waiting for, the nameless something that we are all waiting for. The gods love indirection, they say, so here's a joke: A little girl goes to a restaurant with her parents. The waiter comes over and says, "What would you like?"

The little girl pipes up, "I'd like a hot dog." Her mother looks at the menu and says, "I'd like the poached fish."

"Sounds good to me," her father says. He turns to the waiter, "We'll have three poached fish." The waiter bows and goes into the kitchen. Through the swinging door they hear him yell, "Hey, Louis, two poached fish and a hot dog."

"Look, mom," the little girl says. "He thinks I'm real."

That's what everyone is waiting for, to find out that they're real. No other person, even those who love us to the depths of their heart, can do that for us. They will always be working on their own stuff. They will see their own needs in us, their own loves and hatreds, their own personal beliefs. Linny couldn't take me quitting my job because in my shoes she would have panicked. Renee couldn't take me not loving her enough because I had failed to reach into the place where she felt unloved. Cuddihy had no more use for me because I had transgressed his credo that loyalty is more important than anything else.

So it all boils down to this: You have to do it on your own. You have to kneel before love and say, *Wash it all away.* These words may arise in your heart during some dark night of the soul; they may be only a flicker in your mind during a dark lunch break of the soul. Love will notice and start to work. It will take time for the process to wash away all your stuff. But love doesn't sleep. It brings up the old forgotten hurts and doesn't stop until the healing is finished. One day you're done. You're pure again. You become a raindrop leaving a silvery trail down the windowpane.

"Did you say something?" Fran mumbled sleepily. She opened her eyes without realizing where she'd gone.

"I was asking if you'd like to come on a trip." That wasn't exactly the truth. I hadn't been asking anything, only watching her as the last cloudy wisps were being swept out of her field. "I have some people I think you'd like to meet."

Fran wore a quizzical expression. "I guess," she mumbled. Her face no longer looked raw, but I could tell that her mind wanted to be restless, but it couldn't remember how. "I didn't know I was that exhausted," she said vaguely. There was nothing to tell her, really. The darkest part of her energy was gone, but she was still one of those people waiting to find out that they're real. I told her to go to bed early; I would pick her up before dawn. Confused but willing, she watched me from the landing as I headed downstairs.

After I got home I stayed up. My clarity didn't go away. For a wistful moment I wanted the city outside to leap into beauty or at least a little flame. Nothing like that happened. There wasn't any flash to give me a sign. You take that last half-inch step off the end of the banana leaf, and inside you're praying, "I hope somebody catches me." No one does, but in some miraculous way you don't hit anything. Falling turns to flying, then flying turns to stillness.

What do you do when you suddenly realize that you're real? Because that's what the stillness does. It faces you with something you've never experienced before: pure possibility. Your past can never pull you back again; your ego can't grab control; your emotions stop flinging you around. Getting free isn't the end but the beginning.

Then I had this troubling thought. Maybe a man doesn't get to go any further. Maybe the mystery is sweet and adoring for a woman, because she knows how to surrender her heart, but not for a man. I've never met a male who believed that love is as necessary as oxygen. Women hold on to that belief. Not only is love their oxygen, it's magic oxygen because the ordinary kind only keeps us alive. The magic kind redeems you. So naturally love is a god for them, and men must follow where women lead. What if I couldn't do that?

FRAN SLEPT in the car most of the way until we crossed the state line. The winding country roads in New Hampshire rocked the car and woke her up. She wriggled, straightening out the clothing that had wrinkled and twisted around her. "What are their names again?" she asked.

"Dolly and Elena." I didn't mention the possibility of others since they wouldn't be there yet.

"I can't exactly remember why we're going to see them." Fran was sounding a bit tense and suspicious now. Her energy was clouding up fast.

"I want to ask them the secret of happiness," I said.

"You think they know?"

"It's the other way around—I think I do. I just want to see if I'm right."

Once we got near Dolly's, I missed a turn, and Fran looked hopeful when I told her I didn't have a map. She would have been happy for us to get lost. But after a few minutes, we pulled up to the house. Without a masking of snow, its red door was a shock to the eye.

I parked at the edge of the driveway and got out. "Maybe no one's home," said Fran, not seeing a car. Despite her reluctance, she followed me.

When I knocked, I thought Dolly would greet me with a knowing nod. But when she answered the door, she looked baffled and cross. I mumbled something vague about coming ahead of schedule.

"I was about to eat lunch. The burners aren't working," she grumbled. I told her I'd take a look. She shrugged and turned away, barely giving Fran a glance. What had I been thinking to show up with a stranger without calling ahead? Dolly left the door open behind her. We followed her through the front of the house, which was completely quiet.

"Where's Elena?" I asked.

Without turning her head Dolly said, "Who?" Fran gave me a look. The kitchen was cold. A saucepan was standing on the old gas stove with an open can of tomato soup beside it. I flipped the knobs a few times. There was no hiss of gas. I told her that the pilot light was out.

"Do you charge for that opinion?" Dolly asked sarcastically.

She turned to Fran. "There's tea in the pot. It's cold, but you're welcome to it." Fran shuffled her feet and looked nervous. I found a box of matches and lifted the grate over the burners to get at the pilot. They were black with soot, and the cold air kept making the matches go out before they could do any good.

"I can go to town and get a fire starter," I said lamely.

"Maybe it's the gas main. Did you look outside?" Fran said without the slightest interest. Not that it mattered. I knew who Dolly really was: She was the last wise woman holding out, playing a game with me. Was it perversity? Was it to teach me a lesson or simply her habit of hiding? I didn't care if Fran overheard; I leaned over and whispered at Dolly, "Stop doing this."

Without whispering back she said, "Sit down. You're no help at all." Her impersonation of a feeble, dotty crone was pretty perfect. Hearing her scold me made Fran tense. She took a few paces, then lifted the lid off the teapot and stared doubtfully at the cold brown liquid inside. What was I supposed to do? What was the next step after seeing someone's energy and trying to change it? Then it hit me, the factor I had kept denying: *It's all about you.* If Fran was miserable and baffled, if Dolly was acting impotent and confused, that was irrelevant. I had to change myself. It didn't take a voice to tell me; the stillness inside told me. It had the power to alter any picture as easily as one alters a dream. Nothing was stopping me. So I had a thought and held it there.

Fran emitted a stifled yelp of alarm. My head swiveled to where she was looking. A tallish man with curly black hair was standing in the door. Fran went white, and her limbs began to shake. That was the only part of her that was moving; the rest seemed paralyzed.

The intruder didn't say a word. I didn't recognize him, but it wasn't necessary. I knew the only image that mattered to Fran was Mitchell. Her soul wanted him to be there; I just gave a little push. The man took a step forward, and Fran put her hands up to her face.

"Knife?" said Dolly in a cheerful voice. She held up a large carving knife. I hadn't seen her pull it out of a drawer. "We're so short of suitable implements," she added regretfully. Fran's mouth gulped for air. I knew she wouldn't grab the knife, and I knew Mitchell wasn't real, because his image flickered faintly. But he was totally real to Fran—she was exploding with energy. Tangles and wisps of gray and black flew in all directions. Her heart blazed bright, and then the light radiated to the rest of her body.

Tears were streaming down her cheeks now; she shuddered. I was fairly awestruck, remembering how I had felt when I was in her place. Maybe she would flap her wings and yell, *Whoo-ee, whoo-ee!* Probably not, but I never found out what she did, because the next thing I knew someone had grabbed my arm and was pulling me out of the kitchen.

ELENA HELD on to my arm until we were out of the house and standing on the front steps.

"You got someone over the threshold," she said. She didn't look amazed or radically impressed. It was more like telling me that I now belonged as journeyman to a choice profession.

"Is that the same as carrying someone over the threshold?" I said. A giddy remark, but I was overjoyed to see her.

"It could be. Not that you haven't done it a thousand times before. I'd think your arms would get tired."

Elena looked wonderful. She had on the same green sweater as when I had first taken her away from here. Her eyes were heavy lidded, as if she had been far away before coming to find me. My heart wasn't pounding right then. The stillness that had found its way into the center of my chest prevented that. But a faint fluttering signaled something in my stomach, and when I noticed it, the muscles tightened into a knot. I fought to keep the good part going, but the tightness knotted up. I had an image of Fran freaking out back there.

But what can I say? In the end, the only thing that was wrong was that nothing was wrong. Wait till you experience it.

Have I changed that much? I thought.

"You wanted to help," Elena said simply. "That's been true for a while, only now you want it from a deeper level. The power of desire increases as you get closer to the source." She gave me her patented sidelong glance. (*I must ask her one day if that's a trick I should get in on,* I thought.) "Do you want me to take care of that knot?" Without asking, she gave a small wave of her hand and the tightness in my stomach vanished. I was grateful to be back with someone who could read my mind and sweep away my stuff.

Elena was amused that I was speechless. "You're our poster boy. I knew we didn't make a mistake. Everything can be shaped by love. Sometimes it changes slowly; sometimes you just trip over it." She didn't have to keep explaining, because I saw what she meant. We all want to break through. We all want to have enough passion and intensity to decide our own destiny. But this is such a deep desire that we barely touch on it. We don't share our secret heart even with ourselves.

I didn't think of it right then, but later I remembered a Zen saying: *First a bowl of green tea, then something else, then a bowl of green tea again.*

Which means: Your life is going along, then something explodes into it, then your life goes along again. A wildfire is waiting to break the bounds of ordinary life. Once it does, you get to live the mystery, and no one is the wiser but you and God. In my fantasy, the fireworks never stop; you walk on water and the radiance follows you everywhere. But this Zen way is more beautiful. Your life blends back into the world, and someone hands you a cup of tea. It feels the same in your hand, the shape is the same, the liquid inside will burn your tongue if you don't blow on it first. So what? The tea has become a fleck of the mystery. You see it through the eyes of the soul.

"Now you know how we live," Elena said in the level voice I knew well. "We haven't been keeping to ourselves because we were afraid. Nobody was waking up. We were like mothers to a sleeping world. Do you think anything will change?" She asked this with genuine uncertainty.

"What about what you wrote on my picture?" I said. *"The god of love is back."*

"Well, he was back for you." Elena started laughing, and I asked her why. "It's those priestesses in the woods," she said. "You kept worshiping them a long time. But it's kind of sweet. A lot of men see us in worse ways."

Looking at Elena, my feelings for her went through a change as subtle as the mouth of a river merging with the sea. I had accepted that she would never fall in love with me. And it's not why you think: I didn't stop being attracted to her. I didn't start loving everybody in the world. I just looked at her energy and saw that Elena didn't have any. There was no white light, no centers, no streaming vibrancy. She had disappeared. If I shut my eyes, I could faintly sense that Elena was there, but it was like a note on a flute heard so far away that you couldn't tell where it came from.

I wanted to wrap my arms around her, and so without asking, I did. My hand went to her cheek, I leaned forward without worrying whether she would pull away, and our lips touched.

Only then did I get it. Elena hadn't ever been pushing me away. She had been waiting. This was the only right moment. As she gently met my kiss and returned it, I could absorb who this was; not one woman I wanted for myself but someone who *was* myself. Our breaths softly mingled, and because I had already disappeared as well, I could finally be one with Elena as what she was: love itself. The tenderness that watches and waits.

This is the nectar.

It wasn't a taste anymore. It wasn't tantalizing or tempting or seductive. The sweetness that I had craved was in us both, and we kissed beyond desire. We kissed as sweetness flows to sweetness, as a touch caresses itself. In a flash too quick for images, I saw the thousand ways Elena and I had found each other before, like birds darting through a garden at twilight, touching our wings and parting, being apart to increase our hunger, then touching again to satisfy it, until hunger was past and we could breathe without ache or longing. She had waited for me to find this moment in myself, and once I did, it would endure as long as I endured.

"Take me as yours," I murmured. "Take me as you."

"I already have."

A MOMENT LATER, the world returned. Dolly came out of the house leading Fran by the hand. Dolly didn't divulge any details of what she said to her or how she had reacted.

We more or less had to pour Fran back into my car. Whatever needed to happen, had happened. Fran's energy was blazing like a six-hundred-watt bulb, but she didn't lose it on the way home. She was entranced by awe. She drew some deep sighs, and only when we were getting close to Boston did she say in a husky voice, "Who *are* you?"

I'm nothing that became everything.

These words flashed into my head, but I didn't say them out loud.

"I'm just somebody who came along at the right time," I said.

"I doubt that." There was a wry note in Fran's voice, but it was faint compared to the awe. "What's going to happen to me?"

"I don't know. Would you really want me to?"

"No, I'd rather be a floater." Fran laughed at the word that came out. "A floater," she repeated. Whatever images came into her mind, we both knew that she had survived the quake.

I could see a little bit ahead, could envision Fran boiling over with questions when she came down. I promised to be around. But just then I wanted to get back to New Hampshire as fast as possible. Stepping out of the car, Fran found a note in her coat pocket.

"Dolly must have stuffed it in while you weren't looking," I said. "She's tricky."

Fran tried to read the note out loud, but she was too emotional. She handed the paper to me in the car. It read:

To my newest daughter,

What happened to you today didn't come from me. You have wanted this for a long time, and it is you who made it happen. If only you realized how fortunate you are, because you are about to experience the aspects of love that few people see.

> *Love is what cannot be lost.*
> *Love is what changes the past.*
> *Love is what makes one out of two.*
> *Love is what denies fear.*
> *Love is what fills the holes.*
> *Love is what speaks in silence.*
> *Love is what lets you be seen.*

Save this note, and read it whenever you doubt yourself.

All my blessings,
Dolly

"You probably should keep this around," I said. "You're lucky. All I got was a wad of money."

I thought maybe I should help Fran upstairs, but she wanted to enjoy the feeling of needing nobody to catch her. She wobbled a little going up the front steps. That's what it's like when you're somewhere between falling and flying.

I TURNED AROUND and drove back to New Hampshire. Once I was out of the city, I stopped at a gas station and dropped some coins in the pay phone. Matthew answered, and I asked if I could speak to Renee. Maybe he wasn't thrilled, but he called her and she came on.

"Hello?"

"It's me. I'm on the road. I just wanted you to know that you might not see me for a while. And I wanted to hear your voice," I said.

"That's a funny thing to say. You sound like your regiment is shipping out or something." I let the comment go.

Renee sounded good. We were still friends and we would always care about each other, but that wasn't why I called. I wanted to give us one more chance to be something more. I wanted to hold back the curtain. In case I had made a mistake.

"You there?" she asked.

It was as if I were looking at her from afar, and it was a mixed moment. I saw the beauty in her, and between us, but it was wrapped in a package now, sealed and never to be opened together.

"I'm here. Pretty much all here," I said.

She must have been into this guy Matthew for real, because she didn't run with my opening, either. But we hadn't lost how easily we meshed, and that would never go away. With a flick of awareness, I swept out some of the roughness in her field. There were some pretty bad rips and tears, and one long splinter that had my name on it. I pulled it out and hung up. Renee didn't say

"Love you" as she got off. I knew that was temporary—she would again.

THE WHAT-IFS about my future hadn't solved themselves, but I would take the bowl of green tea. Which means I was going to put on the disguise of being disguised. I'd know there had been a transformation inside, but no one else would. The next time Linny phoned me, I would go back to being the brother she loved to worry about, not the one who had really scared her. She'd never see or hear of Elena again. I don't know about more Thanksgivings around her table, but if I showed up, I'd try and clear some of her jagged energy first. Also, I'd drop in on Cuddihy and ask for some freelance work. He'd grumble, but he'd take me back.

When I came up the driveway, Dolly and Elena were happy to take me in. We made dinner and saved the leftovers. Dolly and I stared at CNN for hours at a time, usually with the mute on. I slept on the couch and felt the morning dampness seeping in through the walls.

On the third day the others began to show up. They were all types of women, driving all types of cars. No sirens, goddesses, witches with familiars. A few wore black; more wore jeans. Some had braided gray hair and no makeup; one had a tattoo (she was nineteen and the youngest). Ten had arrived by noon, not saying much to each other or to me.

I wasn't treated like an outsider or a mascot, just someone they could all assess immediately without much small talk. I wondered how many there would be in all, but we didn't stand around dipping chips.

When the time came, Dolly led us back into the woods. I was in the front with her, helping her over the exposed stumps and fallen logs. Elena and Gloria were close behind us, and maybe six or eight others followed. We arrived in the glade, which was bog-gier than before. Most of the snow had melted off, and the thaw-ing ground made the marble statue of Amor tilt on the edge of toppling. I righted him again and joined the circle the women had made.

One of the older ones I hadn't met, who looked like every-one's Aunt Jane, with hair pulled back in a bun, started intoning. Within a few seconds, the rest of the women joined in:

We stand together in a sacred place
That is nowhere and everywhere
That has ever been and always will be—
The place of our love.
Let us gain wisdom in this place
And be worthy, Spirit of All, to meet here again.

The women paused for a moment then dropped their hands, but I was only dimly aware of this, because with each second the scene was changing. As on the day I'd arrived, the bare branches broke out in buds, the frozen muck became a green meadow. Spring was back, only this time the glory held.

"Step in," Elena invited.

I didn't know if she meant everyone or just me; my mind wasn't all that clear. But I went inside and suddenly I was alone. The glade was gone or had expanded to the far horizon. I saw spring in all directions, and I recognized where I was. Arcadia. The green immortal earth was as pure as the day of creation. Nobody had to dream it into being—the daughters of joy had watched over this garden and kept it perfect, using the same energy you and I were given. Only we have been marking time, while the daughters of joy are harvesting it.

I could hear the women laughing, their voices lightly carried on the soft, warm air. Wherever they seemed to come from, I would walk in that direction, then they would be coming from somewhere else. If life is a puzzle that leads each of us back to paradise, there's a better puzzle awaiting when you get there—you have to figure out how to leave. I never did. I'm throwing you this remembrance of me, someone you once knew, Linny and Renee and the others. Even when you see me again, you won't be seeing me, for I've learned how to be everywhere and nowhere. That's the true Arcadia and eternal spring.

Since I couldn't catch up with the women's laughter, I lay down, and a funny image came to mind: I saw wives kissing their husbands and heading off for an afternoon at the mall, an hour on the courts, a weekend at the spa. But they never wind up there. They meet where no one notices, to remind each other, year after year, of one thing: *Keep living the mystery.*

Some of those who leave home never return. What they experience opens their eyes too much, and they slip away forever. But the few who vanish must be rare. Everyone else comes back as if nothing unusual is on their minds. The SUV pulls up the driveway, the groceries get unloaded, and the kids start yelling for attention.

But these women know something no one else does. They are the mothers of a world not yet awake—but stirring in its sleep.

epilogue

THE STORY ENDS here, but not what Dolly taught me. I returned to the house with the red door many times. I met people at every stage of awakening. If my story seems incredible, consider this: You are living some version of it yourself. I don't look at people the way I used to. When I get on a plane and walk down the aisle, I see incredible patterns of energy. Maybe that's a dry, abstract word, but what are you doing every minute but thinking, acting, and feeling? It takes energy to do those things. Dolly taught me to connect everything back to the source. If you don't do that, you think and act and feel without a true vision of who you are.

"Life itself is tender," she said. "Just as our own hearts are tender. Life is full of beauty, just as our world is full of beauty. Life is intelligent, just as our minds are intelligent. To deny yourself love means that you deny yourself tenderness, beauty, and intelligence."

There are many ways to use the energy you're given. Six billion people have found six billion versions of today, and there will be six billion more tomorrow. Yet strangely enough, there is only one pure way to live today, so six billion is a misleading number. Imagine that you're holding a thread in your hand, and if you follow it, the thread leads where you need to be. The thread begins at your source—it connects you to your soul. The thread leads into the unknown. You can't change the fact that the unknown lies ahead, no matter how much you grasp about the past. Life is like driving a car with a rearview mirror but a brick windshield; looking backward won't help you move forward.

"If you try to use the past as a guide to the future," Dolly said, "you will be guessing. Tomorrow will have some things in it that are just like today. The same family, the same job, the same house. As a guess, if you treat tomorrow like today, you won't be far off. But this isn't what it means to follow the thread that you hold in your hand. The thread leads to a unique tomorrow. The things that stay the same basically take care of themselves. Habit and routine have little engines inside that keep them going.

"The real thrill in life lies with the X, the mysterious things that will be totally new tomorrow, totally unknown. The X is real, but what is this unknown here to teach? If you are four years old, it might be learning how to read. If you repeat the way you always do things, you won't learn to read. For a twelve-year-old, the X will be new emotions. For a twenty-year-old, the X is learning to be an adult. In all these examples, the X is easy to accept, because everybody around you understands how a person develops. Your mother will teach you to read, your peers will affirm your feelings, and society will show you what it means to be an adult.

"But love has always been an X that is unteachable. If you suddenly fall in love, no one taught you how. Repeating what you did yesterday won't make you fall in love today. Even if you turn to someone who has already been through first love, their experience isn't the same as the real thing, which is passionate and alive, unique and powerful.

"If we only knew it, every day should cause that same feeling. Because today is just as unique as falling in love. The energy flowing into you contains the same passion and power. Yet somehow the intensity isn't there. What can be done?

"You have to remake yourself into a lover. Not someone who has fallen in love with one desirable woman or man, but a lover who has a passion for living. Your soul wants you to be this way. It will show you how to find the intensity hidden behind the mask. There's a lot to get past: routine, habit, false beliefs, low expectations, countless hurts from the past. But love can surmount everything. This isn't a sentimental wish; it's science. A science of joy."

I knew about this part. Because love wants to find us, it sends clues every day. The X whispers, *Here I am. Can you see me?* Maybe you're out walking and a bird alights on a fence. The sun catches its feathers a certain way, and maybe the bird's bright black eye notices you. In that instant you hold your breath. Something is saying, *Aren't I perfect? Could I ask for a better moment?* That's the X; that's the mystery. In hints of beauty and silence and stillness your soul gives you a clue. It wants you to pick up the thread that will connect you back to your source.

"Once you notice a clue, your energy centers will begin to respond, as a seed responds to watering," Dolly had told me. "These glimpses of the soul are so delicious that you want more. So even if you think you've forgotten the taste, you haven't. Some part of your mind is always looking for more. Your inner self, which is your subtle connection, is paying attention even when your outer self is conducting business as usual. Desire is the most powerful thing. It wants what it wants. Maybe you wander for a long time wanting this or that other thing, but nice as these things are when you get them, you grow bored. Your inner self has to figure something out. It must stop looking at *things* as the giver of happiness and find the *essence* of happiness."

Let me stop and explain what Dolly means by essence. Imagine that you've fallen in love. You see your beloved, and being completely infatuated, you think her hair is perfect, her eyes are perfect, and her skin is perfect. Are you in love with those things without her? Of course not. You love them because they give you something to look at. It's your beloved whom you really love. This is easy to understand, so go a bit further. You own a luxury car, and being infatuated, you say "The color is perfect, the ride is perfect, and the fenders are perfect." Are you in love with the parts of the car?

Almost everyone would say yes. But actually you are in love with X, the same X that makes your beloved perfect compared to all other women. After all, you must admit that other women could be more beautiful in every detail, but to you they aren't. Because you actually love the essence. This is true when you fall in love with a person, and it's true when you fall in love with a luxury car or chocolate truffles or a new baby or anything else.

Dolly said, "This essence is the nectar of life. Your soul wants you to taste more of it, and you know you want more of it. So the process is like a twin of itself. Love seeks you, because the essence is always flowing as life flows. And your desire reaches out to find the essence. This is like wanting to fall in love, but it affects everything in your life, not just your relationship to one other person."

Maybe Dolly makes this longing for a taste too clear and simple. When you're in the thick of it, of course, it's hell—a delightful hell, wild and explosive when your desire is aroused. The X disturbs everything. It ruins your sleep; it makes your job seem hollow and pointless. An ache of yearning, which you hid so well riding the bus to work, suddenly erupts and makes a mess. The explosion may be soft and sweet, like velvet or warm caramel. It may be like breaking out of jail. Whatever you call it, the X erupts because nothing is more important than the essence of love. In our sane moments we all know this; we're just pretending that having a nice life is good enough.

"The process begins to transform you," Dolly said, "by throwing off the things that don't count in getting what you crave so deeply. Defenses don't count. Negative emotions don't count. Self-image doesn't count. What do these have to do with love? Nothing. So your inner self looks to your soul and says, *Wash it all away.* Of course, you could be kicking and screaming. On the outside, you don't want to see your defenses collapse, your precious self-image erased. It doesn't want to surrender a thing. You've built up this perfectly good self-image, these thick defenses, and a heap of negative rubbish you'd just as soon forget about uncovering. The process won't leave you alone. If love is the real thing at the heart of life, then you must throw away what is unreal. Having tossed out all the substitutes that brought you a bit of happiness and all the excuses for not being fulfilled, you wind up with *what is.* The real thing and nothing else."

There's the gist of it. But Dolly knows that people have doubts. Because the ego-self keeps on kicking and screaming, the process needs to be reinforced every day. One old thing goes flying out the window; another old thing goes flying out the chimney. Your ego-self is screaming, "Hold on! We need those things." But the process won't stop. It stirs up doubt and resistance every single day. Dolly called this part "the journey of return."

"Once you've had a breakthrough, it looks like clear sailing," she said. "Just as when you fall in love, you can't imagine anything ahead but bliss. It feels so free to fall in love. You run ahead, arms wide open, and all the unloving parts of yourself get left behind. You wave good-bye and rush thrillingly into your perfect future. That's the moment of tasting the bliss, shall we say. Its energy can last only so long, however. As your sight clears and you realize that you must live in the everyday world, bliss is still possible. To have it, you must return to all those stranded parts of yourself that you left in the dust. Oh, how you wish you didn't have to look at them again! All that ugliness. So much shame and guilt and humiliation that you never deserved the first time. Some stragglers are whiney and weak, like bedraggled orphans. Some are puffed up with self-righteousness and pride like cheap con men. There is anger and rage, anxiety and dread—I couldn't name the countless bits of your normal self that haven't been uplifted by love.

"But unpleasant as they are, if you go back and give them love, they add to your bliss. The journey of the return brings reconciliation. It brings a ripening. It brings acceptance of who you are. Because love isn't saying, *Come to me when you're good enough and I will cherish you forever.* It's saying, *Bring me everything you are, and I will make it worthy to be loved.* The journey of return is what makes you real, and once it's done, you remain real forever."

Each of us is incredibly complex inside. In a single day, you experience a complete world inside yourself. To make the process simpler, Dolly lumps all the unloved bits together as stuck energy— past experiences you carry around as the toxic residue of the bad things in your life. The energy of being rejected by someone you love. The energy of going through a humiliating interview. The energy of doubting yourself and feeling abandoned. All these energies remain stuck in each of us. The process roots them out and remakes them. Where darkness once was, now there is light.

If the daughters of joy are to make a difference, it will be because Dolly passes on the *mystery* of love. Not love as a feeling, not love as romance or family bonds, but love as the power to turn darkness into light. When Dolly says that anyone can be transformed by changing their energy, almost nobody gets that the process is independent of everything. You can go on with your ordinary life while the process does the secret work of the soul. Not that you won't notice. You will observe everything, feel everything, absorb everything. But you won't control it. Your role is simply to surrender and receive.

I have spent many hours lying on the sofa before Dolly's fire asking her over and over to explain more of this mystery. The subtle world and its invisible actions are things she can see clearly.

"Love is so intimate. It's not like anything else," Dolly said. "Yet love is so powerful and precise at the same time. It can turn a person's life upside down with one glance. Ordinary things get filled with passion. That's just the surface of what is going on, however. Deep down, love is a subtle energy. It binds everything. Unlike physical energy, which is dead, love is lively and awake. When you love someone, you see everything wonderful about them; they become vibrant. A mere touch feels like electricity shooting through you. So that's the second level, just beneath the surface.

"Go deeper and love changes again. It becomes cosmic, what I call the glue of the universe. It plans and organizes. It keeps everything from flying apart. There's another level for you, but go deeper still and something new happens. Love weaves time together, so that everything happens when it should. And finally, when you get to the source, love is your soul. It is the essence of everything real. Since your soul is your part of the divine, at the source you can create anything. The divine is another name for the creative force that silently observes everything with supreme love and intelligence."

"Does a person have to experience all these levels?" I asked.

"To attain your divine self, yes. But have you looked up at the sun through a tree in summer? You see the leaves rustling together, making an ever-shifting pattern. Sometimes they blot out the sun entirely, but that's only for a flicker of time. Somewhere in the canopy the sun is blindingly bright, while other places it is faint and shadowed. There is everything from pure white to black, and the patterns are never the same twice. You are like that. In everyone's makeup the energies shift constantly, sometimes hiding the light of love, sometimes allowing it to come through faintly or in shadow. That doesn't change *what is*. In the deeper reality, love is eternal and constant."

"Then it's up to us to see it more clearly?" I said.

"Yes, that's where the process comes into its own. Once you glimpse the radiance, which is always there to be noticed, you start removing all those shadows and blots that hide *what is*. Now, let's say you want to cooperate. You look at yourself and you decide that you want to allow love to remake you. Your ego, which held out for so long, now says, 'Show me the job, I can do it.' Your mind says, 'Tell me what the problem is, I can solve it.' Your emotions say, 'We feel good about this, but we're also confused and scared.' None of them have the answer. If they did, you would already be transformed. So don't let your ego drive you, don't let your mind think it has figured everything out, and don't let your emotions get discouraged. Any means that uses force, strain, harshness, discipline, demand, willpower, or struggle will be working from unlove."

"Why do you say 'unlove' instead of evil or hatred?"

"Just as unreal is the opposite of real, and makes clear the difference between them, unlove is the opposite of love and makes clear the same difference. Unlove is like illusion, it comes and goes, it changes shape, it tempts you or threatens you. In the end, none of it matters. Either there is love or there isn't. We bypass the whole debate on whether there is cosmic evil."

"Is there?"

"Don't worry about it. The barriers inside you that block the flow of love are less than cosmic," Dolly said.

"But don't you have to feel there's something wrong with you in order to change?" I asked.

"We aren't talking about ordinary change; this isn't self-improvement. People spend years trying to love themselves and overcome the defects they see in themselves. Rarely is that done out of love for oneself. It is usually motivated by dissatisfaction and criticism of the self. How can love be found in that?"

"We all dislike the bad parts of ourselves," I said.

Dolly gave a rueful laugh. "If only you could hate hatred as much as you sometimes hate yourself. Now you see how tricky it all is. Wisdom is shy, like love itself. You can use your energy to try every other means to arrive at change. Love watches and waits. I'm not saying you will be denied love. But many people who feel that they already have love are living on the surface—they haven't touched the mystery yet."

"When does the mystery stop being shy?" I asked.

"When you're ready; when it's your time."

"Can you make yourself ready?"

Dolly nodded. "Oh yes, you can align yourself with the process, as it were. Which means you can change your energy. Love is the force that enters you every day as energy. If you use it well, you will become aware that there is a reality beyond your small individual life. I think the fancy word for this is epiphany, but really it's like lining up the dominoes. One day your energy is lined up so that you are no longer so far away from reality, and then its radiance shines upon you."

"Tell me more about such experiences," I said.

"Oh, there are so many. Hasn't everyone read poetry, heard beautiful music, been moved deeply by nature? Haven't they read their scriptures and listened to miraculous tales? All you have to do is say, 'I wish this for myself. I want to see.' The cosmic intelligence never misses such messages; they come through loud and clear."

"Come now, Dolly, if it was that simple, everyone would be having spiritual experiences. But they don't."

"The reason isn't that love has abandoned them. I don't believe that saying, *Many are called but few are chosen.* Everyone is called; everyone is chosen. But you have to open yourself and receive. To receive, what is necessary? Well, if you wanted to receive a TV signal, what would you do? You'd make sure the set works, then you'd plug it in. The same is true for you as a receiver of life energy. If your set is broken, repair it. This means find the places damaged by unlove. There are certain feelings that immediately tell you that you are thinking or feeling or acting without love:

> *Whenever you feel fear.*
> *Whenever you hate or react with anger and hostility.*
> *Whenever you doubt yourself as someone who is loved and cared for.*
> *Whenever you blame someone else.*
> *Whenever you feel needy.*
> *Whenever you feel victimized.*
> *Whenever you want to defend yourself or punish another.*
> *Whenever you judge or reject anyone else."*

"My God, none of us will ever get anywhere!" I protested. "How can I shed all anger, fear, and judgment?"

Dolly got a canny look in her eye. "You can't, so give up in advance. You see, giving up is the best way to become open. There is no mystery about that. Yet there is a right way to give up and a wrong way. The wrong way is very familiar to everyone: You just say, 'I can't do anything about this. Just let me do what I do. I give up.' Nothing good comes of that attitude. The right way to give up is to say, 'I have lost touch with my source and my soul. I call on them to come back.' And they will, believe me."

"Is this like prayer?"

"Well, it's like prayer but with a follow-up, and the follow-up is big. Every time you think or feel or act from unlove, you have to call yourself on it. Even if the harsh word has already been spoken, even if your judgment and rejection have hurt someone else, you must recognize that unlove was at fault. If the world is going to be yours, the problems are yours, too."

"But you just said this wasn't self-improvement. I'm confused," I said.

"It's not self-improvement because you don't say to yourself, 'I am wrong, I am bad, I am guilty'—none of that comes from love. The secret lies in this magical thing called energy. All energy can be moved. It is malleable. Let me give you an example. Here are three levels of reaction to the same situation: You find out that someone cheated you, and you get very angry. It turns out that there's nothing to be done; the person will get away with it. You can handle your anger by blaming that person and feeling righteous about your rage. You can accept the situation and try to let go of the anger, but knowing that you are right and the other person wrong. Or you can understand that your energy caused you to be cheated, and therefore you take full responsibility to move that energy. In doing so, you actually thank the person for triggering you, because without that person you would not have discovered this bit of unlove inside yourself."

"No way!"

"I told you wisdom is shy," said Dolly. "You will try the first two reactions over and over. In the end, you will notice that you haven't stopped getting angry and you haven't stopped running into situations that give rise to anger. One day you will notice that these two things might be connected. *Maybe something in me creates the situation. Maybe the outer is only mirroring what I am inside.* Wisdom has made a tentative, timid appearance in your mind."

"And the process begins."

"Perhaps. It takes a long time to truly believe that the outer world is a mirror to the inner. Because the way we were all raised, that's just impossible. It can't be that every single thing is *me!* There is no other way to receive love at the deepest level, however, because all reality has one source, and it is in you. If you go outside yourself, you only get further from the source. This is another grain of wisdom that comes to everyone in time."

"Then does the process begin?"

"Yes, if there has been at least a bit of a breakthrough. Nothing happens by accident. You don't have to run out in the middle of the road and wait for a breakthrough to run over you. If you do the inner work, moving all the stuck energies of anger, hostility, fear, and rejection, love will find you automatically."

"Sometimes you make it sound as if I have to change everything about myself, and sometimes you make it sound like the opposite, as if love does all the work and I do nothing. Which is it?" I asked.

"Both. You can't create love when it's not there, no matter how hard you work at it. So in that sense, love does all the work. But love can't reach you unless you move your stuck energy and change all your fears, doubts, and judgments. You work from your side and love works from its side. The channels have to be opened up. Unexpected things will happen, unpredictable choices and possibilities. This varies from person to person. The only certainty is that your life is a perfect mirror. If you alter in the slightest, your outer reality will change simultaneously."

"Can you be more specific about the work we do from our end?"

"Become more aware. Every chance you get, become more aware. I don't mean set aside an hour to meditate and then get up saying, 'I did enough work on that for today.' Every minute is meditation, because at every moment you are aware of something. When you catch yourself being offended by a street beggar, putting down a salesperson who didn't wait on you fast enough, returning one rude remark with another, ignoring someone you love, or starting an argument—common, ordinary things—do two things. Stop the negative behavior, then go and move out the energy. Move it until you feel as good as you possibly can. Don't ask the impossible of yourself; be gentle and never harsh. Some energies have dozens of layers. Fear, for example, is like ten inches of concrete, so expect to return to it over and over. But even knowing that, you must not let stuck energies get away with their view of life. Call them on it. You know what is good and right. When you fall into what is bad and wrong, move the energy."

"How do I do that?"

Dolly paused, as if I had asked a much tougher question than I thought. "Imagine that you are a single point of light inside a knotted ball of yarn. Thread after thread is tangled up at every conceivable layer. These threads are the knotted old energies, the burden of unlove that you carry around. To add to the difficulty, let's say that if you jerk hard on any thread, it makes the ball of yarn tighter. The tangles will only come undone if you work gently and with patience."

"And if you know which one to pull," I remarked.

"Exactly. In a ball of yarn with ten thousand tangles, which one should you pull? You can't possibly know, can you? So you must ask love to show you. This is what is called surrender or what I called the right way to give up before you even begin. Only love knows which is the next thread that needs to be pulled out. And which one is it? You will know from the reflections in your life. The next thing that triggers you to feel negative is a clear signal from your soul: *Pay attention, here's what you must look at.*

"Now you see how the two sides work. Love brings you something to work on, and you do the work. It is all on the energy level. You don't fight the reflection or criticize it or judge that you don't deserve it. The ego likes to offer the same reaction to anything negative: *I don't deserve this, why is it happening to me?*

"The answer is: *Because love says you have to clear it.* Whenever you clear the tiniest bit of negative or stuck energy, a miracle happens. Love comes in to fill the space. You will feel this. New insights will pour in, new solutions will dawn. Problems you thought you could never solve turn out to solve themselves. I spoke about the many levels of love's power, from the superficial to the deepest, which is at the level of your soul. The result you achieve will depend on which level you reach. If you clear your fear a little bit, something will improve superficially. You might feel a little better for a few hours. That is still a result; you have cooperated with the power of love. Next time you may clear your anxiety deeper, and in time it will be gone. Then you will look around and declare in amazement, *Was I ever anxious and afraid?*"

"Let's say I do as you say and await the next thing that triggers my negative energy. At the moment I feel this energy and see that it is unlove, what then?" I said.

"You ask for love to change the energy. Do this in private; close your eyes and go into the fear or judgment or anger, whatever it is. Ask inside what is going on. You will hear all kinds of complaints, all kinds of negative cries. Just be with them. If you are willing, cry and shout and growl, whatever the feeling wants to do. Thrash and move if you want. Don't force, but *do* persist. At first you will feel inhibited—that's all right, since stuck energies always want to hide; they like where they are living. Be patient with yourself, yet put all your inner stuff on notice: *All of you are going to be washed away.* When you get to know yourself well, moving this energy becomes second nature. We already knew how to do it as children, didn't we? Anger made us yell, fear made us cry, and frustration made us lose our patience. As an adult you must get back to that state, not of being a child, but of allowing energy to flow."

"How much work are we talking about? Do I have to devote my whole life to it?" I asked doubtfully.

Dolly laughed. "You don't like the idea of rooting out all the termites hidden below, but it must be done. You can do as little as you wish. Some people want to reach the goal as quickly as possible; others want to relax and not rush anything. Love is happy to do anything you want. I don't mean this is love's only interest in you. The normal joys and rewards of life will continue to come your way. These are the aspects of love you already know how to receive. What I'm calling the process opens you up to receive more. If you do not observe your life getting richer in fulfillment, the process hasn't really begun. This is certainly true if you feel any kind of self-attack or self-criticism. The energy of unlove causes that, never love itself."

SINCE DOLLY'S DOUBTERS weren't there in person, I asked her all the questions I thought they would have brought up. That's how it started. But the daughters of joy go out and help lots of people. They seem to show up exactly when someone needs a flash of insight, a helping hand over the threshold of the soul. After a while more people came to see Dolly, and their questions replaced mine. Sometimes she gave a long answer, sometimes just a hint. In the end, nobody went away thinking Dolly was a hopeless idealist. If their doubts weren't gone, at least they got a good shakeup.

What is energy? Why do you say it can do everything?

Energy is what makes life alive. It infuses dead matter with order and beauty. It binds all the random pieces together so that a lump of molecules can suddenly feel and know things. Energy is the choreographer who stands offstage and organizes the dance. It is infinitely intelligent and aware.

But it's not mystical. Everyone uses energy every day. The flick of desire causes the whole design of your body to change. If you want to lift your hand, a hundred million cells instantly cooperate. How do they know that you want something? Your desire turns on the cosmic switch. You have a different energy when you want to remember what day it is from when you want to go to sleep or want to ask a woman's hand in marriage. Life energy is infinitely flexible; it offers no barriers to whatever you want.

The life force inside you can accomplish anything, but it's not allowed to. Desire keeps repeating what you wanted yesterday but didn't get enough of. So much energy is frozen up in outworn yesterdays that the juice isn't strong enough to make much that's new. What most of us don't realize is that if you go deeper in yourself, energy has an invisible source that is very powerful. When you imagine a rose in your mind's eye, you are doing all that it takes to make a rose. That part is mystical. You have to learn to stop seeing things "out there" as foreign to you. In reality there is an invisible thread connecting your thoughts to everything in existence.

If I lose my temper, I am releasing energy, right? So why do you say that anger is stuck energy?

Because your anger comes back. If you truly release any energy, it leaves for good. Once you know the difference between giving in to anger and letting it go, the process becomes easy and natural. Strong trapped energies are dense and layered—you can't expect to release the whole amount at once. If you patiently keep faith with the process, however, the densest energy can be cleared permanently.

So is stuck energy just another name for feeling negative?

Feeling negative is a symptom that some energy is refusing to move inside you. When you obsess or feel frustrated, when your mind races with ideas or has restless anxiety in it, you know something must be stuck. Deeply frozen energy is more difficult, because it can be numb. Shock is difficult in the midst of crisis, because your ability to deal with the energy is temporarily paralyzed. Terror and fear also paralyze. Any conflict you can't resolve points to stuck energy. Indecision and the inability to commit are much the same.

So you're basically saying that I'm full of this tight, tense energy that I haven't been able to release.

Yes, but that's not a personal criticism. Everyone who isn't seeing their desires come true is blocked the same way. Think of all the times we block out, deny, reject, blame, and resist. These actions, whether mental or emotional, show that we are stuck. Something tight inside us wants to defend itself. It says to whoever comes close, *Don't you dare touch me.* Often there is much ego shielding of this stuck energy. By ego shielding I mean the tendency to control or to be demanding, to find fault with others, to get lost in self-righteousness, smugness, and certainty that you are right.

People who run after external solutions—money, status, sex, power over others—have not yet faced their stuck energy inside. The same is true, strangely, for introverts and depressed people, who can barely face the outside world. They constantly look inside, but that isn't the same as being able to release what they find. To suffer inwardly is a prime symptom of stuck energy, because having failed to release it, you become resigned to the misery of living with feelings you don't want.

What does it feel like when energy is flowing?

You feel carefree and alive. You are relaxed and ready to meet any situation. That's the ideal. On the more mundane level, having a good day means energy is flowing; having a bad day means it's stuck. Although it takes work to move energy, the process is natural. When you laugh you are moving energy. When you find a way to release tension or express love or discover what you really feel like, energy had to move.

Can I talk about my problems and release the energy that way?

If you talk and can come to a place where the energy wants to move, then yes. But many forms of talk, such as complaining, blaming, nagging, and expressing self-doubt and confusion do little more than point toward the energy. You generally will find that talking exposes what needs work, but the real job of moving the energy lies at the emotional level. Stuck or blocked energy is always something that feels bad when you get down to it.

I find myself crying for no reason. Is that good or bad?

It's not helpful to label your emotional states good or bad. Depressed people who barely move the minimum of energy often find themselves sad to the point of crying. But people whose energy flows in a good, healthy way may cry because old, sad energy is coming up to be released. In one case the sadness is stuck; in the other it is moving out.

What about body work that is supposed to move energy through touch or massage? Can this be helpful?

Yes, especially in two cases. If you are so contracted that you can't move any energy at all—this happens during deep depression, anxiety, grief, or denial—someone can dislodge the thicker, dark energies in your body by physical means. At the opposite extreme, if you are deep into the process and need help on subtle levels of energy, someone who knows how to delve into the subtler aspects of the body can be of great benefit.

What is the subtle world? Where is it?

The subtle world is the blueprint of this world, written in mind-stuff. Every object and every event is born first as a subtle image, then as a solid object. You could also say the subtle world is the womb of creation or the home of the soul. It's not far away but right here. If you follow your own energy, you will get to the subtle world. The way you'll know it is that things you think start to come true, desires start to be fulfilled, and you find yourself saying, "It all makes sense. All the pieces fall together." That's just a start, of course. After a lot of practice, you get to be very good at knowing what's going on, like me. (Laughs)

Can you measure subtle energy scientifically?

Can you measure Mozart scientifically? Can you measure your love for your child scientifically? Science operates in the material world and can see almost to the frontier of the subtle world. Yet with all the science in the world, one cannot measure beauty or truth. Every form of subtle energy is already well known to you and needs no proving, because each is crucial to you as a human being. A list of subtle energies would include hope, beauty, truth, compassion, ideals, affection, empathy, intuition, insight, altruism, inspiration, and faith. Tell me when any of these are measured by science, and then ask yourself, Didn't I already know they existed anyway?

How do I know I have a soul?

You can't prove it mentally. You have to have an experience. You can't prove the scent of a rose mentally, either, but when you go where roses grow, the air is full of the scent. Your soul is like that. Its garden is the subtle world. Go there and you will catch the fragrance of your soul immediately.

Sometimes I hear a voice in my head that I think is my soul talking to me. Does the soul speak to us?

The soul's voice is silent. It sends impulses from the subtle world in every conceivable form, because life energy is soul energy. You can't wish, dream, desire, hope, or love without an impulse from your soul. These are its words.

I accept that I wake up every day with a certain amount of energy to use. Why do you say it comes from love?

I feel how sweet and loving the energy is. Anyone can experience that. If you keep looking outside yourself, you won't find where the sweetness comes from. You'll think that a certain person is the object of your love. Or you'll love the taste of chocolate. When you turn inward, though, you get a shock. You find out that the sweetness of love doesn't need any person or sensation. It's part of life. Being is a state of love. It can't be filtered out, so whatever gets created has love at its core, even the ugliest things. But you shouldn't worry about proving this—just follow the bliss until you get to its source. All love, life, and energy merge at the source, which lies in your own awareness.

If the energy that I use every day comes from love, why don't I feel that love all the time?

You could, but you are carrying your past around with you. A baby looks very blissful, but as you leave your mother's arms, what happens? You have experiences, and you begin to split them up into things you like and things you don't. You start chipping up the endless flow of love into certain experiences you are willing to let in and others you're not. All these choices are stored in memory, until in time you have changed completely. Instead of being a blissful creature who lets in the flow of energy, you become critical. Channels get blocked, barriers set up. You avoid potential hurts and imagine what an experience will be like before it has happened. In reality nothing has changed—your soul is sending you an endless flow of energy. But you have caused it to dwindle. Fortunately, like water trying to break down a dam, love is always trying to open the channels again. If you let it, every bit of past limitation can be changed.

Can negative energy turn to positive?

Not really, but it will seem like it. You have to undo the negative energy first, which means changing your beliefs, criticisms, doubt, and judgment. There are a lot of twists and turns to negative energy. Once you start to unravel the knots, however, you find out something miraculous. There is only one flow of life, and it is love. It was your choice to twist this loving energy into unlove. Now you can choose to have the current flow naturally, as one life-supporting power.

There must be something that isn't energy.

Nothing is energy until you see it, feel it, and know what is happening. Everything is energy when you gain full awareness. This has to be so because life cannot exist except as energy. Remember, we are speaking about subtle energy.

Why does love hurt?

Love never hurts. What hurts is the fear of not being loved, insecurity about not deserving love, or some other resistance. Love is the greatest purifier, so it can stir up buried wounds, and then these hurt. It can't be said, however, that love itself causes pain, because the essence of love is bliss.

Why do two people fall in love?

Their energies match. When this happens, they feel as if they have merged. Two become one. Usually one person feels a need that the other fulfills without being asked. The match is automatic, and for as long as you permit the beloved to fill you with energy, the flow of love feels much greater than when you were alone.

Do I have a soul mate?

As long as you are here on the earth you have six billion soul mates. (Laughs) But if you mean, is there someone out there who is completely perfect for you, the answer is yes and no. Yes, you can have such close compatibility that love flows without friction between you and your beloved. But no, it won't be perfect unless you both work to move your unloving energy. The most perfect compatibility is subject to change, and although you may find a soul mate who meshes with your own spiritual evolution—and vice versa—this is almost a guarantee that you will be working through deeper layers of hidden negativity than others who love less profoundly.

People sometimes say "I love you, but I am not in love with you." Is this a valid difference? Should I be with someone who isn't in love with me?

Being in love with someone means you have a passion for them; loving someone without passion is different, of course, and most of us wouldn't want to marry someone who lacks that special passion. But there is a deeper level here. Being in love is unique, because it makes you feel that you have been completely fulfilled by another person. The whole focus is on what the other person is doing for you. In reality that person isn't doing anything. Love comes *through* people; we are the vehicle for a cosmic force that upholds all of life everywhere. Falling out of love can mean a lot of things. The perfectly matched energies start to grow apart. This always happens over time, because when you become intimate with a beloved, your energy is aroused in all the centers. Hidden tendencies are awakened, and if these make you feel more incompatible or less caught up in the rapture of romance, another phase must begin in order to regain that rapture. Being in love has to change from a rose in bloom to a fruit that ripens slowly, abiding through rough and smooth weather.

In an abiding relationship, love becomes stronger because the partners help each other through the process of dealing with all this welling up of energy. Having seen every mood, every fear, every desire of your beloved, you develop compassion, which is deeper than being in love.

I have never found God. Does that mean I didn't love Him enough?

You have found God. When you came to this beautiful green earth and opened your eyes, you found God. He was in your mother's face.

How do I feel God's love?

Any love you feel is God's love. Life itself is God's love.

Is it possible to be loving toward everyone?

Yes, the most loving thing you can do for anyone is to accept where they are on their journey.

If someone needs punishing, can that be done out of love?

No. Punishment is handed out by people who behave from unlove. Often this is rooted in anger, rage, the need to control and dominate, or misguided righteousness. If you are loving, you don't punish. If you are loving, you don't need punishment, either.

Sadly, there is so much unlove right now that the punishers and those who need punishing have no trouble finding each other.

Someone I love deeply abuses and mistreats me. He has a bad background and problems with anger. How should I love him without being mistreated?

Isn't self-love the issue here? You cannot see yourself in a purely loving relationship; therefore, you get the relationship you can see for yourself. What is he giving you that you cannot give yourself? There must be something, or else you would not remain with him while he mistreats you. He is filling a need that is part of your own lack of love. He exposes your lack of self-love by getting away with hurting you. If you don't have enough self-love to know what to do, ask someone who genuinely loves you and follow their advice. Don't be surprised if they tell you to walk out.

I love someone but we fight a lot. Does this mean we are unloving?

Yes. Relationship is a mirror of the self. If your partner makes you angry, he isn't the cause. Your own hidden anger has created this reflection. When you see this, you will stop fighting, because you will know that it's your own energy that must be healed and you who must do it. When you fight anyone, you put blame for your own energy on another, and that is not loving. Of course when you can't help yourself and the energy is too strong, you will fight. Forgive yourself and keep your mind on the reality that this is your own energy being reflected back to you.

Is there such a thing as a relationship without conflict?

All relationships will be without conflict when you have worked through your energy. That's what the process is about. Love is purifying you of everything unloving. Keep this vision in mind. But as you work through the energy, you will experience conflict. Deal with it in as healthy a way as you can, and ask love to resolve the conflict. In time all conflicts can be melted away by the power of love.

What is a love-hate relationship?

A sign of deep conflict. Other people may trigger your unresolved energies. But they are never worthy of hate, nor is hate the darker side of love. I'm sure you've heard it said that we always hurt the ones we love. This is habit, not a law. We hurt those we love because they are so close to us that they stir our deep, hidden energies. Once you own your energy, you will not hurt anyone you love. You will see them in the light of compassion instead.

Are we genetically programmed like other creatures? Perhaps love is just primitive behavior surfacing from the past.

Every person is born with a genetic design, but this design did not create itself. It was created by all the experience that humans have had for millions of years. As we learned, we wrote our lessons down in the form of genes. The universe keeps a journal of how life is coming along. When you want to call upon the past, your genes provide a guide of what has worked over time. But when you have new desires, genes can't hold you back. Desires come first, not genes. Love has the power to rewrite the past.

Can someone be taught to love?

Of course, or else we'd all sink to the lowest common denominator. You teach love by how you handle your energy. Others observe and learn—or not, if that is what they choose. You can also free someone of stuck or warped energy. They won't see you do it, but suddenly more love will flow into their lives.

Why can't love prevent evil?

Love prevents evil a million times a day; prevention is the equivalent of stopping what hasn't happened yet. Love constantly works to purify your energy; it never stops trying to unravel the knots of unlove at every level of your being.

I suppose the sadder question is "why can't love prevent all evil?" This is due to free will. As long as someone believes that unlove is a way to live, no force in the universe can change him against his will.

Why does someone choose evil over good?

You can answer this by asking the opposite question: Why does someone choose good over evil? Because good makes you feel connected to life in countless ways. It adds meaning, it accomplishes positive things, it feels good, and it brings peace among people. To choose evil must mean, therefore, that you are cut off from life, because no one would give up these advantages unless there was no alternative. Since evil is a form of blocked energy, it can be undone at the energy level.

If someone is doing something you know to be wrong—or even evil—can you change him back to good?

You can influence a person back to good by your example, and you can improve a person's energy if you know how. After that, everything depends upon the person's own will. Changing someone who isn't willing to change is impossible, even if you love that person from the depth of your heart.

What if you have been so hurt in the past that you are afraid to love?

What you are afraid of is your own fear. Fear is an energy, so if you deal with that energy, love will come to you naturally.

If you want a loving relationship, how do you go about finding the right partner?

There is no need to. Love is seeking you. Already it exists in your life at the highest level you are permitting. If you work on your energy, more love will flow through you.

Is sex an expression of love?

It depends. Sex is like every expression of life—it can be connected to love or disconnected. At its source, sex is nothing but love. It is the creative force of the universe. Sex between two human beings becomes involved in everything else. You can imbue sex with any other feeling; you can imbue any other feeling with sex. If you want to use sex as pure pleasure, nothing wrong is occurring, but you will usually find that you have isolated sex into a mere sensation. Sensations don't increase the value of life; they don't connect us with other people, because a sensation is completely private. To use sex as a connection with others, you have to blend it with love, self-worth, respect for others, kindness, joy, and giving. These values are what make you human, and they will make sex more human as well.

You make it sound as if there's a science of joy.

There is! (Laughs) The most important part of joy is a mystery. We will never know why the creation has infinite joy at its heart. We will never know why joy feels the way it does. We will never know why joy makes us expand to the point that we are imbued with the divine. But once we see that this eternal mystery is before us, we can learn how to take part in it. The science of joy is just a map, a way to get from where you are to the goal of feeling joy.

Is joy the same as ecstasy?

If you find a difference, please tell me. I want whichever one is best. (Laughs)

Have you ever seen God?

Don't be embarrassed, but I see Him looking at you.

Can energy be so twisted and warped that love can't fix it?

Energy can choke itself off so completely that the person has no memory of love and no motivation to find love. These are rare cases. When they happen, it is nearly impossible for an impulse to touch the person's heart. Such a person is cut off from the source and lives in darkness. This darkness can take the form of evil, despair, hatred, or mental illness. No one is in a hopeless situation, but in these cases, the atmosphere would have to be so full of love, so pure and clear that there is no room for wrong behavior. With no outlet for the darkness, it would begin to wither, and little by little, openings would appear for the light.

If something bad happens to me, does that mean I don't love myself enough?

Like attracts like. Anything in your life that is without love has arisen because you attracted it from inside yourself. However, that doesn't mean you don't love yourself. It means that you are human, and to be human is to contain thousands of bundles of energy. They will range from the highest to the lowest vibration. Each one will attract an event in your outside life that mirrors it. When the event appears, you have a choice. Either you fight against the reflection or you work on the energy that caused it to show up. If you fight the reflection "out there" without seeing to the energy "in here," a similar event will come back your way sooner or later. If you work on your energy, the event will return only to the extent that you haven't fully worked through the energy.

I was in a destructive relationship that I managed to finally get out of. If I work on myself, will the next relationship be free of this kind of destructiveness?

Destructive relationships exist when two people mirror negativity to each other. If you work on the negative energy, it can't attract its reflection. Automatically the next relationship will not have to mirror quite so much back to you. There is no guarantee that you have done enough work to get a totally loving relationship. The guarantee is that no amount of work will go unrewarded. This itself is a gift and a miracle. To think that all you have to do is change a little energy, and automatically you attract more loving people and more nourishing situations.

When you say "Work on your energy," what exactly does that mean? How do I do that?

There is no fixed formula that holds good for all of us every day. Working on our energy begins wherever you are with your emotions. Look at yourself and ask honestly what feelings are facing you at this moment. The most obvious negative ones can't be missed, whether they are depression, anxiety, fear, hostility—whatever you see before you at this moment. For it is in the moment that all work is done. You will revisit old emotions, certainly, but the doorway is always what you feel now.

The actual work consists of doing what it takes until that particular feeling loses its grip. I've mentioned the techniques, ranging from breathing to physical acting out to emotional expression. Start with the one that strikes you as right. Don't delay, don't deny, and don't minimize your feeling. It may take you hours to process a momentary rush of anger or it may take a few minutes; no one can predict.

Just know that emotions aren't random. They are offered up as needed for their clearing. The inner and outer world are matched. Every moment is a step in your growth. I know this sounds as if processing can become a kind of all-consuming mission. You don't have to make it that. Seek instead to have a loving relationship with the person inside. Would you reject the offering of your closest friend? Your inner self is infinitely dearer than your closest friend, so stop disregarding what is brought to your attention. With every bit of energy that you move, you open a small link of communication with your soul.

Can I work on my energy all at once?

Life is set up to bring you every needed situation in its own right time. You don't have to attack all your energy at once. Just deal with the reflections that come your way today. Believe me, you will have your hands full!

I want my children to experience more love than I did. How can I do that for them?

Children can't be trained in energy work, and they shouldn't be. Provide care and nourishment, and above all work on yourself. As a parent, every step of progress you make will be reflected in your children's lives. This is a precious time. Once they embark on their own experiences, their energy will be sealed off from yours, which is how it should be—only by themselves can they forge a meaningful life. During their formative years, however, children take their energy cues almost entirely from you, and to the extent that you can allow the energy of love to flow through you, they will gain as much as you do. This is another miraculous gift we can all take advantage of.

Why do men seem more unloving than women? Aren't they responsible for most of the violence and lack of love we see in the world?

The problems we see in the world are not caused by men but by distorted male energy. No one can deny that violence and aggression have become a dominant male trait (not ignoring that women can have their own typical issues with anger). What causes this distortion? Why did men decide to dominate with such cruelty and selfishness? You don't have to find the answer. All you have to do is heal the male energy. When in balance, a man can be as open to the infinite flow of love as a woman. The only thing that will be different is the flavor, because the father god and the mother god give rise to different but compatible traits. If you are a woman, a man is fascinating because you sense the difference. If you are a man, a woman is fascinating because you sense the difference. If either energy becomes distorted, then there is a deep, destructive split at the very heart of human nature. It's a grave problem, yet the solution is the same as for any energy. In one way we are fortunate, because drawing the opposite sex to us comes naturally; the attraction gives more incentive to change than if energies that are trapped deep inside the ego have no outlet in sight.

I've heard that the most a woman can do for a man is to love him. Do you believe this?

Not if it means giving the same love that hasn't worked in the past. The most a woman can do for a man is the same as what a man can do for a woman: Work on your own energy and support the same work in your partner.

Why are so many women enablers?

Their center of power is so closed that they feel powerless without a man. When they solve this problem by finding a man to take care of them, they get the bitter with the sweet. The man who protects you also dominates you. Your will cannot influence his, so you have little choice but to keep supporting him. When a victim supports a dominator, the result is called enabling. The end of enabling comes when you fix the energy blocks in your power center.

Religions seem to teach that men have more power than women and have thus led to the subjugation of women. Why has this happened?

All religions come in two parts: the holy words and the history of how those words are lived. Holy words are those that show us the way back to our source; they are guides for connecting the material world and the world of the soul. The sexes are equal at the soul level; therefore they deserve to be equal in religion. The fact that women are subjugated belongs to that other part, the history of how holy words are lived. It's up to you if you want to join any tradition or history. All are littered with many distortions of energy, many deviations from love, many abuses and inequalities. You also have the choice simply to follow the holy words and win your own soul's freedom.

How is lack of love related to sin?

Lack of love causes distorted beliefs and actions. If your energy is so distorted that you can't find a loving way to act, you will be considered a sinner in many religions. But not all. Every faith has left room for compassion, and in the eyes of compassion a sin is like a child's misbehavior. You do not mistake the sinner for the sin.

If you are in a situation that involves violence, is it better to work on your energy or to leave?

Almost always it is better to leave first and then work on your energy. Violence will increase the negative energy and make it harder to work on. Fear deprives you of the strength and will to work on energy. You can't be tender with yourself in a house of violence. And then there's just the practicalities: Energy work takes time. Healing the deepest negative energy is a matter of months and years, not days and weeks.

Define loving behavior. How is it achieved?

Accepting yourself and others without judgment. Judgment is a negative belief system held in place by stuck energy. You judge someone as wrong in order to feel better about yourself. As long as the energy remains stuck, so will the judgment. You need it, because you can't find the real way to feel good about yourself, which is by being open to the flow of love. If you get the energy unstuck, love can reach you. You will begin to accept who you are, and automatically you will have no reason not to accept others.

What is unconditional love?

Unconditional love is that which is completely free of unlove. Unlove comes from stuck, distorted, blocked, and warped energy. So if someone tells you that they love you unconditionally, either you have met someone who has done many years of work on themselves or you have met someone with a kind heart who has a habit of wishful thinking.

Name one thing that doesn't depend on energy.

I can name as many as you like. The soul doesn't depend on energy nor does anything that comes from the soul, such as truth or compassion. The issue of energy enters the picture only when you get to the material world, where nothing can exist without energy.

When I was growing up, hate was the opposite of love. Now people seem to say that fear is the opposite of love. Why?

Hate is the emotional opposite of love. It is negative attraction as opposed to positive attraction. Fear is the spiritual opposite of love. Fear causes the centers to contract, making it impossible to receive love, power, or insight. When you are deprived of these impulses from your soul, you can't feel love. You are cut off in a world of unlove, a world where beliefs are shaped by fear. It takes a longer line of reasoning to get there, but this is the reason fear is considered the opposite of love.

I don't feel afraid or anxious. I'm not angry or hostile. But I can't say I feel the flow of love. What's your explanation?

You're hiding from yourself. Being afraid or anxious or angry, at least occasionally, is part of being emotionally alive. If you can't feel the negative energy, usually that's a sign that you've numbed yourself. At some level, you've told these energies that they are forbidden to express themselves. Ask the jailers to let everybody out. When you release the negative energies, there's a flow, and only in the state of flow can you return to love. Freezing over won't do it.

Does love always bring happiness?

Yes, but perhaps not in the short run. Love isn't a feeling and is not the same as pleasure. You won't be happy while love is working to correct your distorted energies. But don't get depressed. Allow the process to unfold. Instead of saying "This is my time to be happy," say "This is my time to get real."

Is it possible to be in love forever?

Well, that's the whole point, isn't it? (Laughs)

To Rita, Mallika, Candice, Gotham, and Sumant—
thank you for who you are

To Felicia and Carolyn, who constantly and tirelessly
kept up with the numerous revisions that I made

To Jennifer Hershey, my editor, for her superb editing suggestions

To Robert Gottlieb—thank you for encouraging me to go
in this direction

about the author

Deepak Chopra, long a passionate voice for spiritual re-
newal, is the author of numerous books, which have been
translated into thirty-five languages, nine of which have
been on national bestseller lists. Hailed by *Time* magazine
as "the poet-prophet of alternative medicine," he is the
founder of the Chopra Center for Well Being in Carlsbad,
California.